Gladys Mitchell di[...] a life in which she c[...] writing more than [...] shire, and went to G[...] She began teaching [...] English in 1921, and continued to work as a teacher at various schools in London and Middlesex until her retirement in 1961. From 1929, when she joined the writing profession with the publication of her first novel, *Speedy Death*, she produced at least one novel a year until the end of her life, all featuring her formidable sleuth, Mrs Beatrice Adela Lestrange Bradley.

Gladys Mitchell received the Crime Writers' Association Silver Dagger Award in 1976.

# GLADYS MITCHELL

*

## *Sunset Over*

## *Soho*

SPHERE BOOKS LIMITED

**SPHERE BOOKS LTD**

Published by the Penguin Group
27 Wrights Lane, London W8 5TZ, England
Viking Penguin Inc., 40 West 23rd Street, New York, New York 10010, USA
Penguin Books Australia Ltd, Ringwood, Victoria, Australia
Penguin Books Canada Ltd, 2801 John Street, Markham, Ontario, Canada L3R 1B4
Penguin Books (NZ) Ltd, 182–190 Wairau Road, Auckland 10, New Zealand

Penguin Books Ltd, Registered Offices; Harmondsworth, Middlesex, England

First published in Great Britain by Michael Joseph Ltd 1943
Published by Sphere Books Ltd 1988

Printed and bound in Great Britain by
Richard Clay (The Chaucer Press) Ltd, Bungay, Suffolk

# CONTENTS

*

# BOOK ONE

## Rest Centre

*

Here needs no Court for our Request,
Where all are best,
All wise, all equal, and all just
Alike i' the dust.
Nor need we here to fear the frown
Of court or crown:
Where fortune bears no sway o'er things,
There all are kings.

Robert Herrick

---

### CHAPTER ONE

## *Blitz*

Mrs Bradley gave the raid an hour; then she went the round of the shelters which she was scheduled to visit. By the time she got to the Rest Centre the raid was at its height. Gunfire and bombs provided its orchestra, and searchlights, flares from the enemy planes, the brilliant pyrotechnic bursting of shells and the lurid light from buildings already burning, sufficed to illumine a scene from the inferno.

Mrs Bradley had become interested in the effects and results of air-raids. Noise stimulated her. She did not connect, she found, the crump of bombs, and the whistling shiver and thrill of their descent, with an active and virulent enemy, but regarded the raids with the objective interest she would have felt for natural phenomena – hurricanes, earthquakes and landslides.

She was amazed, however – although it had already become a commonplace – at the extraordinary calmness of the people.

7

Their courage did not so much surprise her, for she was accustomed, in general medical practice, to the staggering philosophy of humanity; but their acceptance of the appalling din and danger was, to a psychologist, unexpected and very interesting.

The Rest Centre, part of the premises of a Baptist Chapel, was in Maidenhead Close, and by the time she got to it some dozens of people had arrived. Their moods were various. Some had lost everything they had. All were, in some degree, shaken and stricken. Mrs Bradley found plenty to do, and the people had plenty to talk about.

'They say the *Cat's Whisker* is down to the ground,' said a man who had been pulled out from under a wrecked shop near Drury Lane. The *Cat's Whisker* was a synonym for a thieves' kitchen masquerading not unsuccessfully as a Soho tavern. 'Bennie seen it bust up.'

He indicated a black-faced, filthy creature whom Mrs Bradley recognized as a young professional boxer who used the gymnasium over the sports shop on the corner of Mild Court, the next street to Maidenhead Close.

'That's right,' agreed this apparition. 'Plug's place, too, where I trains. Come down like a pack of cards, the blooming lot – shop, gymansium, everyfink.'

'And where were you, Bennie?' Mrs Bradley enquired.

'In the cellar. Clawed my way out. Give first-aid to a fellow with a nasty 'and, and come on 'ere for a kip. Staying with Plug while I trains. Called up tomorrow I am, so I thought I better kip down tonight, that's all. Else I'd a stop' there. See?'

His manner was a curious blend of the belligerent and the self-righteous.

'Did Plug get out?' asked Mrs Bradley.

'How the bloomin' 'ell should I know?' demanded the youth. 'Got meself to look after, 'aven't I?'

'And me to look after you,' said Mrs Bradley, nodding. The boy was a tough little Jew called Bennie Lazarus, trained to a hair, and highly-strung.

'Get this man between blankets and keep him as warm as you

8

can,' she said to a St John's Ambulance worker who was standing by, waiting for her orders.

'I'd have got Plug out if I could,' said Bennie, beginning to cry. 'You know that, Ma. 'Im and me was like brothers.'

'If you please, Doctor, could you come over to Mrs Zellati a minute?' asked one of the Rest Centre staff. 'She's got a haemorrhage, but she insists on getting up and going to look for one of her children. They're all here – we've counted and checked them – but she won't believe it.'

Mrs Zellati was lying in the little emergency hospital which opened off the end of the basement shelter of the Rest Centre. Mrs Bradley went in and comforted her, and then was called upon to deliver judgement on the diet of Joseph Guisser, who said he was diabetic.

The people were of all races and classes. There were, on this particular night, Jews, Greeks, Russians, French, Chinese, negroes and English, of all ages and types. The Staff and Officers were almost rushed off their feet, but the service was amazingly selfless, and the people, on the whole, were patient, reasonable and brave.

'We had the St Giles' House at first,' said the Supervising Officer, 'but we couldn't take all those who wanted to come. We shall only use it as an overflow dormitory in future. People were awfully good at helping us move across here. The local people, I mean. Some, of course, were connected with the Baptist Church, but there were others – the sort you'd never think would have put themselves out at all. They humped our bales and bundles, and worked like navvies to get us settled in.'

The Supervising Officer was a slightly-built man with a thin face relieved from asceticism by a lively and charming smile. He was a well-known painter, and Mrs Bradley had often admired his work in exhibitions before the war.

The Centre, too, she admired. She felt that the Staff were proud of it. Certainly the results of their work were striking. Imagination and good taste had gone to the planning of the Centre, and the rest and recreation rooms, the dining-room and the rooms for the children's games, all had their separate characters and were comfortable, bright, interesting and pretty.

There was neither an institutional smell nor an institutional air about the place; the lounge was tastefully furnished; the pictures were good; books on top of a long low cupboard against the end wall opposite the windows gave a pleasing and friendly effect. There were flowers on a table, a carpet on the floor; curtains, apart from the usual hideous black-out blinds, to the windows. A large and comfortable settee occupied the short wall opposite the bookcase. There were armchairs about. The room looked homely and yet dignified.

The other rooms were in keeping. There were flowers on the tables in the dining-room; toys in the children's playroom. The planning of the rooms for their various uses had been a triumph, also. The kitchen opened into the dining-room; the dining-room into the lounge. Between the lounge and the recreation rooms were the Supervisor's office and the Welfare Officer's room. The sleeping accommodation for the people who used the Rest Centre was down in the basement, which had been strengthened to form an air-raid shelter. This dormitory was in two sections, one for men and the other for women, and it had emergency exits in addition to the flight of stone steps which led to the level of the street and to the outer door.

This part of the Rest Centre Mrs Bradley already knew well, and she also knew the small Emergency Hospital which opened off one end of the dormitory, and in which the nursing sister on duty usually sat patiently knitting. On this particular night, however, she had, like the rest, as much work as she could possibly manage.

At last the worst of the night rush was over. More people would come in in the morning when the police had roped off areas containing, or suspected of containing, unexploded bombs. Meanwhile there was a short break, during which the Staff could snatch a cup of tea and smoke a cigarette.

'Well, I don't think it's been as bad as last time,' said the Welfare Officer, handing tea to Mrs Bradley. 'What do you think, Godfrey?'

Mrs Bradley glanced from one to the other of the officers. They were, superficially, a study in contrasts; studied carefully (as Mrs Bradley, interested, had studied them), their characters showed some amazing resemblances as well as sharp differences. But even the differences were not divergent in their nature; they were co-operative, and the resemblances never had the unfortunate effect of producing competition, jealousy or any of the lesser and meaner vices, but merely enhanced and deepened the first impression of solidarity of purpose and essential comradeship of these two people so fortunately in juxtaposition.

The man was not less, but more, a man in that he recognized in himself some of the neater, quieter, more penetrating feminine qualities. He was, in fact, a complete human being, this almost delicate-looking aesthete, Mrs Bradley surmised, and his strength lay in never underestimating either himself or the people with whom he had to deal. He had authority, like the flash of a sword, and humour, like sun-rays coming in brilliancy from behind cloud.

The woman had judgement and courage, as had the man. Her authority was not like his, but seemed to rest upon her shoulders as though it were truly the mantle with which it is sometimes compared. She neither argued, drove, nor appeared to assert herself in any definite way. She was a natural leader, as sure of herself as a rock. She had integrity as well as courage, and the meaner virtues seemed to have passed her by. Mrs Bradley heard that she had three sons, all serving, and could well believe it.

Her humour was not keener than the man's, but was different in quality. She was more acutely alive to the ridiculous, especially as it appeared in people's actions; less acutely aware of the verbal shaft. The man, Mrs Bradley thought, might die for a theory; allow himself to be martyred for an idea; the woman was of the mettle that would plough up the stubble on a battlefield, even before the battle was quite at an end. She was of the pioneer stock, intensely individual, possessed also of great acumen and a mentality masculine in its breadth, feminine in its subtlety; and yet, Mrs Bradley surmised, for a thousand hells in the man's life – fear, pain, self-searching – the woman would never know one. Mental and physical fear lay outside her experience, it seemed. She was self-reliant by nature; the man had learned self-reliance, probably by self-expression in his paintings. He was, pre-eminently, the artist; she, shrewd, humorous, kind, implacable as Nature or Fate.

Mrs Bradley could not help wondering how each would react to some of the experiences which she herself had had of crime; what attitude they would adopt towards murder, for example; whether their notions of justice would always coincide with those of the law.

'Are you tired, Doctor?' asked the Supervising Officer.

'She is weighing us up and finding us wanting,' said the Welfare Officer, refilling Mrs Bradley's cup. 'What did you think of the emergency maternity arrangements, Doctor?'

'Marvellously adequate,' said Mrs Bradley.

When she returned to the basement shelter which was used as the Rest Centre dormitory she found work to keep her busy until the morning. The All Clear was sounded at five.

Considering the length of the raid and the damage done to buildings, the number of casualties was not as large as might have been expected. It was heavy enough, however. She felt tired and depressed, chiefly with hunger, by the time she reached her rooms in Gerrard Street.

Her premises were intact, although buildings at the end of the street had suffered considerable damage.

A youngish man was sprawled in her longest armchair. He jumped up as soon as he saw her.

'Hullo, David,' she said.

'You've been working all night,' he said. 'Lie down and rest. I've got the breakfast ready as far as I can. My lodgings are busted wide open, and I've taken my landlady to the Rest Centre. She's crying her eyes out, poor old soul. Every stick she's got has gone except her potted geranium, and she's clinging to that as though it were her child.'

'I've just come from the Rest Centre myself,' said Mrs Bradley, sitting down and letting him wait on her. 'I didn't see her there, but I talked to the furnace man about the heating before I came away, so perhaps you brought her in then. How is Mr Piojo, by the way?'

On the previous evening a half-breed sailor, a Spaniard on his father's side, had been brought to her surgery. She had patched him up and had transferred him to Charing Cross Hospital.

The young man Harben grinned.

'He's all right. They were pretty fed up with him for getting himself knifed when they wanted every bed for air-raid casualties. He didn't want them to touch your bandages. He thought they had some special magic about them, I believe. Anyhow, he's tough, and a clean-living sort of fellow. He'll soon be up and about. How do you like your coffee?'

'Black,' said Mrs Bradley. 'How did you come to be with him when he was attacked?'

'It wasn't he who was attacked. That knife he took on his arm was meant for my ribs, I think. Someone must have been lying in wait in Little Newport Street.'

'Who?'

'I don't know. He was off before I could reach him. You can't recognize people in the black-out. And now, whilst you get some sleep, what would you like me to do?'

'First, find out what has happened to my friend, Plug Williams. You know his shop, almost on the corner of Mild Court?'

'Is Plug hurt?'

'I don't know. His shop was demolished. Second, enquire for survivors from the *Cat's Whisker*, which also came down last night. Third, go to the Rest Centre in Maidenhead Close, and find out whether they want any help this morning. Fourth, you had better look out for yourself, I should think. Your earlier adventures lead me to imagine that your enemies are particularly persistent, but you have not, have you? – been attacked in Soho before.'

'No, but I live here, you know, at any rate, during the winter. I daresay I have enemies among so many foreigners. A knife isn't English, somehow.'

He cleared away the breakfast things, went out, and returned at noon with his report.

'Dodger, from the *Cat's Whisker*, is in Charing Cross Hospital with a fractured thigh and concussion. They have hopes of him. Say he's got a skull like teak and the fracture is compound but not complicated. Charlie, the barman at the *Cat's Whisker*, is safe, although a bit knocked about. He went to the Rest Centre this morning, and they're keeping him until he finds somewhere to go. The *Cat's Whisker* was his home. They're still digging for some of the customers there, but some have already been rescued. The proprietor was not on the premises. Nobody knows where he is. They think he has made for the safer areas. Plug's shop isn't down. There isn't even any debris. The Rest Centre is busy and is functioning well. They're all up to their eyes, of course, and I did what I could – chiefly washing up and peeling vegetables. Some of the people are in pretty bad shape. They've lost everything they ever had, and don't know how to make a start again. The middle-aged ones are the worst. There's a crippled woman who won't be evacuated with other cripples. Says she likes it where she is, and shall stay. Interpreters are at a premium. They've got two Russian women this morning, several Austrian refugees, some Greeks, a Swede and about a dozen French. Some of 'em understand English and others don't. The officers and staff can do a bit of German and French, but the other languages are constituting a problem.'

'Thank you,' said Mrs Bradley. 'Well, now you may take me out to lunch, and then we'll go back to the Rest Centre.'

They lunched in Piccadilly, and picked their way back to the Rest Centre over broken glass, debris and all kinds of rubble and mess. Demolition parties were already at work, but the business of London seemed, otherwise, to be proceeding much as usual.

At the Rest Centre matters were going well. The patients, except for Mrs Zellati, who, convinced that her children were all safe, had submitted to be removed to hospital, greeted Mrs Bradley, for the most part, with humour and goodwill. The officers and staff were concerned with what seemed to be an eternal coping with Fate in the guise of representatives from the Town Hall to announce that an unexploded bomb had been removed; the District Officer for Repairs, who came to inform the Supervising Officer of the Rest Centre that he had no authority to carry out any repairs at the Centre except those needed for the black-out; a messenger from the Area Office to say that the removal of Elizabeth Halkins to hospital after a previous raid had not been notified to the proper authorities; the arrival of an ambulance to evacuate two old men and a woman who had signified their wish to go into the country; a young gentleman from the department of the Borough Engineer, who had selected this very inconvenient morning to inspect the electrical appliances in the medical room; and a visit from Miss Mollie O'Cann of the Canadian Press, who thought the Rest Centre just too cute and old-world, if she might say so. Then appeared an elderly gentleman who had come to find out the name and address of the caretaker, a younger gentleman who indicated that the church had a claim on the L.C.C. for damage done to the roof in a previous raid, and a middle-aged woman who came to ask what share, if any, the church members could take in helping at the Centre. A quarter of an hour later, a gang of workmen arrived to repair the roof. Questioned by the Supervising Officer, they claimed to have been sent by Holborn Borough Council, and were permitted to proceed.

Scarcely had they begun work when the Supervising Officer and Welfare Officer were called out to meet members of the Samaritan League, who had come to offer their services. As there were always jobs for volunteers at the Rest Centre, for four meals a day were served there to upwards of two hundred people, the permanent staff cheered up, and soon found the Samaritans some employment. Mrs Bradley had tea with the officers.

'Better use my room, Edith,' said the Supervising Officer. 'I've got a small table in there.'

'You know,' said the Welfare Officer, 'we made rather a curious discovery this morning, which I think would have interested you, Doctor Bradley.'

'It has interested the police,' observed the Supervising Officer. 'There's going to be an official investigation.'

'But what is there to investigate?' Mrs Bradley enquired, with a horrid presentiment that she had, by her thoughts, wished something unpleasant upon them.

'Godfrey thinks it's a corpse, but *I* think it's a practical joke. It happened like this: we've a young girl here – you've seen her – who's going to have a baby. She felt rather faint this morning, so, to save her walking up the steps to the street, I went out with her into what we call ... "underneath the arches". Have you been out there?'

'No,' said Mrs Bradley.

'Well, there are some old arches – most mysterious-looking, and a kind of passage – and as soon as we got out there this girl said to me ... "Oh, look! I wonder how that got there! Doesn't it look revolting?" ... or something of the sort. She speaks very broken English. It was a box, really, but it was almost the shape and size of a coffin, and it really made me feel quite excited to see it there, because, you know, I love anything gruesome and mysterious. Of course, I was only playing at having those feelings, but I told Godfrey, and he went and looked at it ...'

'And slightly unscrewed it,' said the Supervising Officer, 'and very hastily screwed it up again ...'

'And now he's told the police. You know, Godfrey, I do call that brave of you. The police are always so sceptical, I think, when the ordinary citizen tells them anything. What do you think, Doctor Bradley?'

The Supervising Officer laughed. There was a close and, to most people, a surprising comradeship between the sensitive, vibrant, almost ascetic man and the practical, self-possessed, lively, dominant woman.

'I'd like to see this mysterious box,' said Mrs Bradley, 'but as you have reported its arrival, I suppose I must wait until the police have had a look.'

When she left the Rest Centre, David was waiting for her.

'What have you been doing since lunch?' she enquired, for they had parted at the top of Maidenhead Close some two and a half hours earlier.

'Oh, hanging about. After all, I live in Soho six months of the year, you know.' Mrs Bradley thought it odd that he should emphasize this point. He added defensively, 'I've lots of friends. I'm here all the time I'm not on the river in my old tub. Why shouldn't I have friends as well as enemies in the neighbourhood?'

He walked back with her to Gerrard Street and said goodbye

at the entrance of the high, old, rickety house in which she had her flat.

She was preparing to mount the staircase when from the floor above descended one of the street-walkers.

'Oh, hullo, dear,' said the girl, upon seeing Mrs Bradley in the hall. 'That wasn't Dave Harben, was it?'

'Indeed it was. Do you know him?' Mrs Bradley enquired.

'Only so-so. Not in the way of business, dear, if you understand. He done a book about me once. Nice fellow, 'specially if you happen to be down on your luck. And don't want nothing in return. Haven't seen Billie, I s'pose? I'm going out to 'ave a look for her. She's not been home all the morning. Cooked her breakfast for her and everything, I did. Always gets home to breakfast from her Wednesday. Gets rid of her, he does, before his lady secretary turns up. Being treated like dirt, I call it. What's a lady secretary? Takes his money, same as we do, that's what I always say.'

'Whereabouts was Billie staying?' Mrs Bradley enquired.

'One of them posh flats off Beau Street. Know 'em?'

'There's been some damage there, I'm afraid,' said Mrs Bradley. 'I hope you'll find she's quite safe.'

'Makes business chancy, these air-raids,' said the prostitute.

Mrs Bradley mounted the stairs, unlocked the door of her sitting-room and then heard a sound from the kitchen. She went up the two wooden stairs at the turn of the landing.

'Have you been here long?' she enquired. It was her old friend Detective Inspector Pirberry of Scotland Yard. He got up from the kitchen chair to greet her.

'Expected me, did you ma'am? Not that I see how you could.'

'No, I didn't expect you,' Mrs Bradley confessed. 'Why, are you here for some special reason?'

'Well, ma'am, they've found something funny at the Rest Centre round in Maidenhead Close, and I thought you might like to be in on it, seeing you are kind of interested round there. The Supervising Officer reported the matter to Gray's Inn Road, and Inspector Dewey there got on to me. Do you care to have a look-see, ma'am?'

'I'll walk round to the Rest Centre with you,' said Mrs

Bradley. 'Have you yourself seen what has been found? I heard something about it half an hour ago.'

'Really, ma'am? I thought you and I would have first look, perhaps. It seems to be a long box, rather like a coffin, and there's no doubt there's something inside.'

'I confess to considerable interest. This box was not in the Rest Centre before the raid, I take it?'

'Well, that's one of the things that would have to be figured out, ma'am. It's getting a common trick to dump bodies where it's hoped they'll look like air-raid casualties, of course, but . . .'

'The person who put this box in the Rest Centre can scarcely have hoped the contents would look like an air-raid victim, you mean?' said Mrs Bradley.

'Yes. Well, they rang up Gray's Inn Road, as I said, ma'am, and Dewey asked me whether I would care to come and have a look. He said it had been put there very recently, as, at six o'clock on the evening of the raid, it had not been there, the Officers were certain. The Welfare Officer gives it out as gospel it wasn't there, because she and the nursing sister had been testing the black-out of the emergency hospital at six, and she's a very dependable lady. During the testing it had not been dark, and the lady seems, ma'am, positive that, had the box been where she afterwards saw it, either the nursing sister or herself would have been bound to spot it.'

# CHAPTER TWO

## *Body*

The coffin-like box, opened in the mortuary, disclosed contents suitable only for re-interment. The police, however, thought it necessary to ask for a post-mortem examination. The result was interesting. In spite of the fact that the body had been dead for – the experts thought – between two and three years, sufficient arsenic was recovered to indicate that death was due to acute arsenical poisoning. The victim was thought to be a man of between sixty and seventy years of age.

'It had to be murder,' said Pirberry, confronted with these sinister findings, 'or else why dump the coffin in such an unlikely spot?' He returned with Mrs Bradley, Dewey and the sergeant to the Rest Centre.

'Good morning,' he said to the Supervising Officer. 'Would you kindly place a small room at our disposal, sir? I shall have to ask your staff a few questions.'

'You had better have the Staff Room. I'll turn them out and put a notice on the door.'

'Thank you, sir. That will do admirably. You can't, of course, throw any light yourself upon the matter?'

'I'm afraid I can't. I went into the basement that morning on a routine inspection, but I did not go into the area. The last time I inspected the arches was after we had them cleared of rubbish when the L.C.C. partially blocked in the top of the area as a safety measure. I know there was nothing there then. After that we put out some junk from upstairs, but the furnace-man saw to all that.'

'I'd better see him first, then. Will you call him, please.'

The furnace-man, introduced into the Staff Room four minutes, later, wiped his hands down the seams of his trousers and said he knew nothing about coffins. There had been no coffin on the premises before Saturday, which was the last day on which he had seen the arches. He wanted to keep extra coke down there, not coffins, and but for the idiocy of the L.C.C. in blocking all possible coal-chutes from the street, he would have had another five ton put down there, ah, that he would, chance what! They could do with it, come winter. As for coffins, he thought their place was underground.

The Welfare Officer came next. She described the finding of the coffin, and could give the approximate time of the discovery. She could not agree that the coffin might have been placed under one of the arches, could not see, in fact, how it *could* have been placed there. There was no way down to the area now except from the shelter, and the door between the shelter and the arches was kept locked. The Supervising Officer had a key;

so had the furnace-man. She herself had no key to the door. She had had to procure the Supervising Officer's key in order to take out Mrs Pibeski, who had morning sickness and had asked for a little fresh air because she felt faint.

'We shall have to find out whether it would have been possible to any unauthorized person to get hold of the furnace-man's keys,' said Pirberry, when the Welfare Officer had gone. 'Meanwhile, we'd better have this Mrs Pibeski, if she's well enough to come up.'

Mrs Pibeski came up in the lift. She was a young, beautiful Polish woman whose English was just – but only just – capable of bearing the strain put upon it by Pirberry's questions.

Yes, she had been sick now several mornings. No, her place had not been bombed, but there was the bomb which did not go off. The police had told her to go away until the bomb had been taken away. It was admirable of the police to concern themselves for her safety. For herself, she did not mind, but there was the baby coming. Her husband was – had been – an airman. He was dead.

Mrs Bradley noted Pirberry's reluctance to introduce the subject of coffins.

'It is strange,' continued Mrs Pibeski, 'to find a coffin in the outside of our beds. Myself, I regard it as an omen. I am alive. I shall die. What do you say?'

'You mean you saw this coffin before Mrs – before the Welfare Officer had taken you into the area?'

'No. When we go, I see. I speak French. She speak French, too. *"Voilà!"* I say. She say yes, she seen it. We examine. I say the church have a crypt. She say yes, certainly. The air-raid had flung up the coffin, and we are there.'

'Thank you, Mrs Pibeski,' said Pirberry. 'You have been very helpful. I think,' he added to the Supervising Officer, 'we'd better see the staff, in order, next, sir, if you please.'

The staff consisted of three women and two men, and the Supervising Officer, a man of modern views, asked which of the five would most suit Pirberry's taste. Pirberry, who was intrigued and astonished by this – to him – remarkable subscription to the doctrine of the equality of the sexes, selected Miss Bond, the most experienced in the Rest Centre work.

'Coffin?' said Miss Bond. 'Well, of course, I've seen coffins, as it were. But in the Rest Centre, no. Not if we have any luck, that is.'

'Thank you very much,' said Pirberry. The other four had nothing to add which could help him. They slept 'all over the place' as Miss Welch, the youngest member, put it, but none of them slept in the shelter, although they went 'down there if the Jerries got too saucy.' It was soon obvious that they had nothing whatever to tell, and Pirberry soon made an end of them, and asked for the Welfare Officer again.

'There's no doubt, ma'am,' he said, 'that I shall have to depend on you for the major part of the evidence. Can't you add anything to what you've already said?'

'I don't think I can,' she answered.

'We may be coming back, ma'am. Will you think things over, and hold yourself at our disposal to answer any more questions?'

'Oh, yes. Why not?' said the Welfare Officer. She caught Mrs Bradley's eye and smiled. She was a remarkably good-looking woman, thought Mrs Bradley, noting again, and with a renewal of her previous pleasure, the decisive generosity of the mouth and the humour and shrewdness of its smile.

'Come out to lunch,' said Mrs Bradley. But the meal, delightful though it proved to be, was productive of very little extra information.

'I'd like to know, as much as you would, how the coffin could have got there,' said the Welfare Officer, at the end. 'But I don't see how anybody could have put it under the arches without our knowledge.'

Her voice was low and soft, and easily audible – a wonderful voice for public speaking, thought Mrs Bradley.

'No?' she said. 'That is the first consideration, of course. I had hoped that someone would throw some light on that. I wonder whether I might come with you back to the Rest Centre, and have a look round for myself?'

'Oh, yes, do come.'

They went first to the Welfare Officer's room. Mrs Bradley

had been in it before, but regarded it with renewed interest. It was high above the roof-tops of all the surrounding houses, and had a square carpet patterned in red, dullish green walls, distempered, a piano against one wall and a camp bed against another, a large cupboard opposite the bed, a writing desk, and, over the bed, a copy of *The Music Lesson* by Vermeer. This was the only picture in the room. The window was in the wall above the desk, and the door was almost opposite the window. There were also two or three chairs.

The room was next door to that of the Supervising Officer, but was entirely different in character and atmosphere from his. One would not have hesitated an instant, Mrs Bradley decided, in concluding which was the man's and which was the woman's room.

'I don't know how much you gathered from the police questioning,' said Mrs Bradley, 'but it seems a clear case of murder.'

'I know,' the Welfare Officer replied. 'And, you know, Doctor, I feel rather terrible when I think how I said I loved mysteries and those sort of horrid things which one usually only reads about. Now it's close home, like this, I almost feel as though I'd brought it upon us myself. Godfrey thinks I'm silly, but I do confess to being a little bit superstitious in these matters.'

Mrs Bradley said she sympathized entirely with the feeling, but that the theory which produced it must be entirely false.

'Well, I don't know,' said the Welfare Officer. 'I could tell you some very queer tales . . . but I expect you'd be able to match them. Hullo, here's Godfrey come to give you the freedom of the city, or whatever you would like to call it.'

The Supervising Officer came in. He was slightly annoyed with the police. The Welfare Officer soothed him.

'And now Doctor Bradley wants to look at everything,' she said, 'especially the place where the body was found. I think I'll come too. She can tell us the very moment she doesn't want us.'

They all went down in the lift and walked through the empty dormitory. Mrs Bradley was reminded of a mediaeval hospital. There was no time to let the mind linger on such imagery, however, and they went out into the area.

There was nothing more to see than Mrs Bradley had supposed there would be. She spent about seven minutes down there, then suggested that they might as well return to the top floor. The area itself had, so far as she was concerned, no tale to tell.

She discussed the affair again, but without any profit, with the officers, whilst they stood in the entrance to the dormitory. Then she interviewed Masters, the Rest Centre furnace-man.

He seemed able to tell her nothing, and would not admit that his keys were ever out of his possession. Later, Mrs Bradley discussed him with Pirberry.

'I'd believe he might know something about it, ma'am,' said Pirberry, 'but, the trouble is, he doesn't admit to a thing. If he were guilty, I should think he'd at least have the sense to tell us he'd lost or mislaid his keys, and leave us to argue that somebody must have taken them and stowed the body away; but he doesn't admit they've ever been out of his possession. That sounds like the barminess of innocence, if you understand what I mean.'

'The Supervising Officer also has keys,' Mrs Bradley pointed out.

'Yes, I know, ma'am, but I think we must rule him out. For once thing, he's a most respectable gentleman. Well known in art circles, and all his life an open book, as you might say. Whereas Masters is a bit of a mystery. He's fairly new here. Only been employed the last three months. The old furnace-man went into the Navy. An ex-chief Petty Officer *he* was. We're taking up this chap's references, of course, to see where that will lead, but it doesn't seem to lead very far. He worked as a gardener in his last place; then he got sacked – he won't say why, and there's nothing in his record to tell us. He was on the dole for a bit after that, and then this was going so he applied, and was picked because one of the congregation of the Baptists recommended him and said he understood the heating. Apparently it's similiar to the greenhouse furnace he used to have as a gardener, only on a rather larger scale. Of course, if we could get the old gentleman identified it would be more than half the battle, but I'm afraid he's too far gone for that, even if anyone came forward and was willing to try, which, so far, nobody has been.'

'Was there nothing at all to go on? I saw nothing but the remains. Had there been no clothing?'

'You're welcome to see Exhibit A, ma'am, but it doesn't seem to help very much. It's been a dressing-gown. We're on the track of where it was bought. Not that that will help much. There are probably dozens like it. Come along, ma'am, and see what you think. I'd be very glad of some help.'

The dressing-gown was preserved in a sealed glass case.

'You wouldn't believe what it smells like out in the open,' said Pirberry with melancholy enthusiasm. Mrs Bradley could have contradicted this statement, but did not do so. She made a drawing in her notebook of the patterns on the material, and, as she did so, gazed at her sketching with a wild surmise which quickly changed to a feeling of absolute certainty.

'I can identify this dressing-gown,' she said.

'You can, ma'am?' Pirberry's voice betrayed restrained but jubilant surprise. 'You mean you know who it belongs to?'

'I can't give you his name, but I recognize the dressing-gown, unless it has been described to me very badly.'

'Oh – you couldn't swear to it, ma'am, you mean?'

Mrs Bradley did not answer this, but suddenly said:

'How else does one get into the basement besides by using the stone staircase?'

It proved that there was no other way. There had been a way, in a sense, before the war, because the arches were under the street and the passage which ran past them, and from which they opened like caverns, had been under the pavement and was covered by gratings through which the passers-by along Maidenhead Close, had they chosen to do so, could have looked down upon the area.

The coffin, therefore, could have been lowered into the passage from the street, supposing the grating to have been removed, but it could not have passed under one of the arches, and, had it been left in the passage, it must certainly have been discovered long before its dramatic appearance after the end of the raid.

It was true that the Rest Centre had a second staircase, but this merely formed a second exit to the street, and did not descend below street level. It was not even intended as another entrance to the Rest Centre, for it was closed by a panic-bar, and unless this had been left open at any time, the Rest Centre could not be reached that way.

Mrs Bradley's tour of inspection led to one other discovery. This was particularly interesting. The church, which was very large, had an enormous gallery, and this gallery could be reached without previously entering the church, for a door half-way up the staircase communicated directly with it. If a hiding-place had been wanted, one might have been found, Mrs Bradley thought, in an obscure corner of the gallery. At least, that was her first theory; she rejected it instantly, however, because she felt sure that the cleaners would have been bound to find anything so hidden, and if they had found the coffin-like box they would have reported it.

Since, on the unimpeachable evidence of the Supervising Officer, the coffin had not been under the arches when the Rest Centre had first been staged in the church rooms, it was not possible at present to say when the coffin had been brought to the building, nor where it had lain hidden.

In the end she was inclined to suspect that the roof might have been used, at least as a temporary hiding-place, for she noticed that at the top of the lift-shaft there was a small landing from which a ladder went up to a skylight.

She returned to the inspector to acquaint him with her findings, such as they were.

Pirberry listened with close attention to Mrs Bradley's remarks, and, at the end, nodded his head.

'I confess I hadn't got as far as putting the coffin on the roof, ma'am,' he said, 'but it did seem to me that it must have been on the premises some time before it got put down into the area. Your idea about the roof is a good one, and could bear investigation. I'll go up myself and have a look. And I'll bear in mind about the repairs. Mind you, the whole thing still turns upon the identity of the body. If we could only put a name to the old chap, we might find his murderer pretty easily. What was that about the dressing-gown, again?'

'I'll tell you, when you've got a your list of suspects,' said Mrs Bradley. 'In any case, it's a story you partly know.'

Pirberry, who was accustomed to her methods, grinned, and said that he could scarcely bear to wait, and would look at the roof immediately. Mrs Bradley elected to accompany him, so they sought out the Supervising Officer and told him what they proposed to do.

The ladder was steep but short. Pirberry went up first, warning Mrs Bradley to mind his feet. Workmen were busy on repairs. The roof was in several sections, owing to the odd assortment of architecture which now made up the chapel, and each section was divided from the next by a path of leads about ten inches wide, so that it was a simple and perfectly safe matter to tour the roof and gain an impression both of the repairs which were being effected and of any possible repositories for a coffin.

'It beats me, ma'am,' confessed Pirberry, when he had toured the whole of the terrain, greatly to the detriment of his suit, for there were occasional crags of roof which had to be negotiated and up which it was necessary to crawl by means of ladders or wooden slats. He dusted blackened hands down his blue serge trousers.

Mrs Bradley had not attempted to go further afield than the section of the roof which was actually under repair, and which happened to be almost over the trap-door. Here she accosted the foreman and asked when the roof had last been repaired.

He was unable to tell her, but stated that it would be put down in the chapel accounts, he supposed. An elderly workman, handling tiles, overheard the conversation, and informed her that he reckoned he could put a date to the last job. It would have been just before the war, in the May. He had been on the work. It had been a small sort of a do. He reckoned he could show her the very part, if she had a mind to see it. He seemed to feel no surprise at an elderly lady's interest in tiles and roof-repairs, and Mrs Bradley had to step the shortest possible distance from where they were standing. The workman walked to the left, in the opposite direction to that taken by Pirberry, and there were the window tops of the offices occupied by the Supervising and Welfare Officers of the Rest Centre.

'It was these 'ere winders,' said the workman. 'Bricks round
'em re-pointed, a lick of paint on the gables and the slates
renewed. There'd been some wild sort of weather, and snow, I
seem to recollect, and they was afraid of tiles slipping down in
the street and killing somebody.'

Mrs Bradley descended the ladder near the top of the lift-
shaft, and waited for Pirberry to join her.

'We're still confronted with the task of discovering which
people could have gained access to the roof without exciting
comment,' she observed. 'The coffin itself was probably lodged
on top of one of those two windows. I think there would be room
if it were placed broadside on. It might be visible from below,
that is the only thing, but I don't know whether that would
matter, so very high above the street, and the street so narrow.'

'Of course, we've no proof it ever was on the roof,' Pirberry
pointed out. 'I must have another go at that Masters, and
another comb through the register of those who used the Rest
Centre that night. But it's the identity of the dead man we want,
ma'am. Once we know that, the rest should follow on.'

On her way from Maidenhead Close to Gerrard Street Mrs
Bradley met David Harben. He had been, he said, to see the
wounded half-breed. He was now almost well enough to be
discharged from hospital.

'And what have *you* been up to?' he demanded. 'Are you still
messing about at the Rest Centre?'

'I have been emulating the devil by going to and fro in the
earth, and by walking up and down in it,' she responded.

'Ah,' he said; he fell into step beside her. 'One thing, I seem
to be clear of all my troubles, unless the gent who laid out El
Piojo has another slap at me. Do you want any help with yours?'

'Mine are not troubles,' she answered. 'I am enjoying a
mystery of a body in a box. It was found in the basement area
after an air-raid, and there is little doubt it had been moved
from another hiding-place, although whether that hiding-place
was also in the Rest Centre, or whether it was somewhere else,
we do not know. I suppose you would not care to help us.'

'I'm not interested in murder,' said Harben.

'Are you not? I thought it had general, if not particular

27

interest. What did you make of the attack on Mr Piojo? Wasn't that murderous?'

'I tell you it was not intended to be an attack on him, but on me.'

'But even if it *was* intended to be made on you, it was none the less murderous, was it?'

Harben did not reply. At the northern entrance to Leicester Square Station they parted. Mrs Bradley walked up Little Newport Street, and when she was almost at the Gerrard Street end of it, two men lurched out from a doorway, fell towards her and would have knocked up against her but that she was much too quick for them. She had dodged them, hooked one round the ankle and left him on his face on the pavement before he could have realized what was happening. The knife in his right hand tinkled against a shop-front. She kicked it ten yards away just as a policeman came up. The other man made his escape.

'There's his knife,' said Mrs Bradley, 'if you want it. Please remember me to Inspector Dewey. My name is Bradley.' She added that she would be seeing Mr Pirberry in the morning.

The constable, who appeared to be somewhat astonished by her manner and messages, led his prisoner away, and Mrs Bradley continued on her way home. She was not molested, although she looked sharply round the unlighted vestibule, switching on her torch for the purpose, as soon as she arrived.

The staircase was old enough to creak loudly on almost every stair. Her fellow-lodgers were, on the whole, peculiar, but they could never move about unannounced. It was one great advantage in a house which, otherwise, had little to recommend it except that it was in the district which happened to interest her at the moment.

Her flat had been used as club rooms until the beginning of the war, and her agreement included a clause by which she agreed to continue to house the club library. She had met the secretary, and had been invited to make what use she liked of the books. As most of them were valuable modern works on physiology, she was interested, and, on this particular evening, when she had had tea, prepared in the tiny kitchen which boasted little in the way of amenities except for a gas oven, a kitchen table, a cupboard and a sink, she took down one of the volumes and settled herself to read.

Her sitting-room overlooked the street, and she had been interested to discover that when the windows were open it was possible to hear conversations from the street if there was no motor traffic about.

Her attention was not wholly engrossed by her book. She was thinking partly of the man who had tried to knife her. She could not say she had recognized him, and yet there was something at the back of her mind which seemed to be trying to work its way to the front.

She was about to shrug these thoughts away, and immerse herself in a chapter on the ductless glands when voices below caused her to put down the book.

She unlatched her sitting-room door and set it ajar, and then seated herself so that she was facing the doorway. The voices passed into murmurings, and the steps began to sound to the tread of heavily-shod feet. She listened. They passed the first landing, from which opened the premises of a family of Jewish tailors; they passed the second landing and the flat where lived the two street-walkers; still they ascended. The stairs creaked, groaned and resounded beneath their tread. A voice – the voice of David Harben – cried loudly:

'Anyone at home?'

'In here,' Mrs Bradley answered. The door opened, and David Harben entered, supporting a badly-wounded man.

'Another acquaintance of ours; the Spanish captain,' he remarked. He stepped aside, and pushed the captain forward. The poor fellow's shirt and coat were soaked with blood, and he himself was half-fainting with pain and shock, and the weakness due to loss of blood.

'Why on earth did you not take him straight to hospital?' demanded Mrs Bradley.

'This was nearer. Only happened in Little Newport Street. Had a fight with his mate this morning at their lodgings, and we think Don Juan laid for him again. Do you think he could possibly stay here? He hates the idea of a hospital.'

'He could stay here if I had anywhere to put him,' Mrs

Bradley pointed out. 'And he could stay here if I weren't afraid of gangrene, and he could stay here if I were certain we weren't going to have an air-raid.'

'I see,' said Harben dispiritedly. He rang up the hospital whilst Mrs Bradley tended the wounded man.'

'And now,' said Mrs Bradley to the Spanish captain, 'what happened? I am interested, because I myself was attacked this evening on my way home, and in Little Newport Street. Do you suppose your precious Don Juan laid for me too?'

'If you please?' said the Spanish captain. Mrs Bradley grinned.

'When are you going back to Spain?' she asked. This question the captain could answer.

'We go – when? There is not a ship,' he said. 'My ship I think you know, has been torpedoed. Not torpedoed. Shot to bits. We were rescued. My mate – he is my second sister's husband's brother-in-law – is the traitor, I think. There were lights. Blue lights. I have heard.'

'Germans?'

'Maybe. We were carrying – I make no secrets – we were carrying rifles. They were for Norwegian patriots. Gun-running. But a good cause. You, who are English, would say so.'

'I suppose so, yes.'

'Juan Hueza is a villain. You remember – Don Juan, my mate?'

'The police will deal with him.'

'You want to know,' said the Spanish captain suddenly, 'whether it is Don Juan who has wounded El Piojo as well as myself. It is not. It is other fellows – sailors.'

'What is the connection between these attacks and the abortive attack on myself? And was the attack on Mr Piojo intended as an attack on Mr Harben?'

'I do not know. I know little of Mr Harben. I did not know him at all until he was shipwrecked near the beginning of the war. You know of that. We picked him up not far from Gran Canaria. How he comes there I do not know. We landed, rescued from open boats, after my ship is gunned, on the south coast here – ship gone, cargo gone, crew gone, except for Estéban and Jorge and also this fellow, El Piojo.'

'That coincides with the story Mr Harben told me,' said Mrs Bradley. The captain bowed.

'Sit down!' said Mrs Bradley sharply. 'Keep as still as you can with that arm. Give him a cigarette, David.

## CHAPTER THREE

## *Preliminaries*

'Well, ma'am,' said Pirberry on the following morning, 'all I can say is, nothing seems to hang together anywhere.'

The raid on the previous night had lasted for the usual number of hours, and both he and Mrs Bradley felt tired, although his younger, ruddier face showed perhaps more traces of fatigue than her older, yellow one.

'One thing struck me,' she said, 'although there's probably nothing in it. Why did Bennie Lazarus tell that lie about Plug Williams' shop coming down?'

'He was pretty well shocked, you know, ma'am. He may honestly have thought it came down on the night he took shelter in the cellar, or wherever it was.'

'Yes,' said Mrs Bradley. 'Again – although it may have nothing to do with the matter we are reviewing – who is it in Little Newport Street who constitutes himself such a danger to the community? Is it really Don Juan, I wonder? Or is it the man the policeman apprehended when I was set on and kicked a knife out of play?'

'The fellow who attacked you? His name is Sidney Ferruci. He swears he wasn't intending to attack anybody. His story is that he was going out to buy a bit of fish, and had his knife in his hand to cut off the bit he wanted. As it happens, the fishmonger, another Italian named Callotti, swears that Ferruci was in the habit of doing this, and says he's as harmless as a dove. What we're trying to prove, of course, is that he's the

31

bloke who attacked the two Spaniards, but he swears he doesn't know them from Adam and certainly they refuse to swear to him, and so does Mr Harben, who seems mixed up in it all. So there we are.'

'Yes,' said Mrs Bradley. 'I did not, at the time, suspect Signor Ferruci of wishing me harm.'

'As for the Rest Centre business,' Pirberry continued, 'I can't get any further at present. I can't find any people at the Rest Centre who can completely alibi themselves for the night of the raid when the body seems to have been put down in the area, and, so far, we've found five shops who sold, before the war, dressing-gowns like the one on the corpse. They were expensive, it seems, but not uncommon. My chaps are still checking, of course, but it doesn't seem to get us anywhere, so I doubt whether your identification would do us much good, ma'am.'

'Are all the shops owned by one firm?'

'Yes, they are. The dressing-gowns were made to a special order, but all the branches stocked them.'

'Are all the branches in the West End?'

'West End or City. Why?'

'No reason. I suppose the dressing-gowns were all sold over the counter?'

'Well, in a sense. That is, they were chosen in the shop, but, naturally, most of them were sent. It wasn't war-time when that dressing-gown was bought.'

'Could I hazard a guess that one of the gowns was sent to an address in or near Chiswick?'

Pirberry stared at her.

'You're not kidding, ma'am?'

'No, I am not.'

'But what made you connect up – ?'

'The pattern of the dressing-gown, as I thought I told you.'

'Someone was very foolish, ma'am, to bring such a clue to your notice.'

'Very foolish, or very penitent, Inspector. Or, of course, completely innocent. But, to return to this question of the box containing the body, don't you think it more than likely that the coffin came to the chapel before the Rest Centre was in being?

And, that being agreed on, don't you think it may have been taken from the roof down into the area for fear of air-raids damaging the roof?'

'Quite likely, ma'am, but I can't see how that would help us. It's still a mystery who brought it to the chapel at all.'

'I'm going to tell you a story,' said Mrs Bradley. 'Some parts of it you know, but only the least important. It concerns David Harben and these Spaniards, and, to a certain extent, the body.'

# BOOK TWO

## The River God's Song

*

Do not fear to put thy feet
Naked in the river sweet;
Think not leech, or newt, or toad,
Will bite thy foot, when thou hast trod;
Nor let the water rising high,
As thou wad'st in, make thee cry
And sob; but ever live with me,
And not a wave shall trouble thee!

Fletcher

---

### CHAPTER FOUR

## Nymph

She lay well up on the slope of the river gravel, a tub-like
structure scarcely worthy the name of boat. About her, and
under her strakes, were the rounded pebbles, the silt of the river
bed, and, further away, the spits of firm sand on which glistened
thinly the light of the rising moon.

The shallow river, streaked with oil from petrol launches and
fed by sewage from the town, ran between banks diverse as well
as opposite. On one side were houses, a concrete path to form
their street, three pubs, some hoppers at moorings, a yacht, two
motor cruisers, four lamp-posts and a boat-builder's yard. There
were also six tiny almshouses built sideways on to the river and
dedicated since 1788 to Six Old Men of the Parish. David
Harben, who lived and worked in the tub all through the spring
and summer, knew the six old men and used to give them
tobacco whenever he sold a book.

On the opposite shore was the towing path; were the willows, restless in their leaves; were the sacks of cement put down to strengthen the bank and to stiffen and maintain a too-precarious footway; was the wooden landing-stage for the small squat river-steamers; was the jetty for rowing-boats and canoes; was even the entrance to a fair-ground from which, on this fine Whit Monday late in the month of May, the blaring of the round-abouts had been heard for a mile down the river.

But all was silent now; and, except for the riverside rats and the young man at work inside the tub, the waterfront seemed deserted. There was no one on board the yacht, and the pubs were closed. Behind curtained windows without one chink to let out a ray of light, the inhabitants were in bed. The six old men slept in their almshouses, and the mallards slept on their nests by the oozy bank. Only in the tub was anyone stirring and awake.

This David Harben was a novelist. If his hobbies had been listed they would have consisted of the words Small Boat Sailing. He was an authority upon pre-Conquest Norman architecture and was no mean swimmer, but small boats were his great interest, and only lack of means (although he was not, as authors go, a particularly poor man) prevented him from indulging his tastes all the year in all the navigable waters of the world.

The tub was his concession to this lust. She was old, decrepit, three-parts home-made, and had as many idiosyncrasies as a retired prima donna; nevertheless, she served the double purpose of summer home and all-weather sweetheart to Harben. He did not so much love her as cling to her. She brought him the satisfaction his books never brought, and she comforted him as only his mother, whom he had lost in his boyhood, might have done. She fitted herself to his moods, controlled and modified his habits, accepted his mastery, could be gay, quick, quarrel-some or downright contrary, and combined in herself all those uncertain, sometimes irritating but always fascinating qualities which a man has the right to expect in the woman he loves.

Harben was thirty-two years old, and a bachelor. He lived, during the worst of the winter, in a room above a delicatessen shop in Charing Cross Road from whose windows it was not possible to see the river. Each winter day he walked towards the Strand and thence to the Embankment. Here, unless it were pouring with rain, he would lounge, stroll, lean, ponder, accept odd jobs on river craft, if any such jobs were going, and get himself carried to Millwall Docks, to Tower Bridge Pier, to Tilbury, to Woolwich Ferry, or even up-river to Battersea, Chelsea or Brentford.

When February was out, and the rivers everywhere were all in flood for the spring, he would leave his dingy lodging, his voluble, charming, tri-lingual landlady, and all his friends on river craft large and small, and get back to the tub once more.

Soho and the Embankment, Leicester Square and Drury Lane, Long Acre, Blackfriars, Shadwell, Blackwall, Deptford, Rotherhithe and the inscrutable Charing Cross Road with its million secrets, were then left out of his life until October ended and the tub was laid up once more.

One winter, after the death of his greatly-loved father, Harben had tried the experiment of keeping the tub in commission all the winter, but he found her too cold a companion and caught pneumonia. Only by using his judgement and catching it early enough and lightly enough (so he told his friends) had he been able, by the following May, to get on the water again. Even then he had lost twelve weeks of a lovely spring.

He reckoned to write not more than one book a year. He was lazy, even for a novelist. He had, as most writers have, a will-o'-the-wisp for guide; the nearer he thought he caught up with his vision of the moment, the more teasingly it seemed to elude him. He was doomed to be perpetually and perennially dissatisfied with his work. He was not a genius. He was a sensitive man of great talent, an artist in the making; unsure of himself; egotistical, self-centred, yet open to impressions, kindly disposed as Abou Ben Adhem, and apt to get into scrapes because of this.

Upon this particular evening, he was completely absorbed. After weeks of semi-idleness, a fit of nervous irascibility brought on that day by the appalling noise of the roundabouts from the other side of the bridge had supplied him with the energy to work. He was visited, as they say, with inspiration. He saw his book suddenly and clearly, and in consequence – for something outside a man seems to take charge at such times – he might have worked on until dawn but for a surprising interruption. It

37

startled him out of his mood, and when he picked up his pen
before morning it was only to check the written pages.

The interruption was not only unexpected, but came without
hint or warning. At one instant there was nothing but the night
all round him, kept at bay by the oil-lamp on its bracket at
the end of the little cabin. There was nothing to be heard but
the almost inaudible sound of the fine pen moving hastily on the
paper. The next instant (with no sound of footsteps to give
warning that someone approached) came the tapping of fingers
on one of the little portholes of the tub.

The young man, startled, screwed the top on his pen, and
turned his head to listen. The tapping came more distinctly.
Although it was still very quiet, there was an urgency about it
which made his heart thump foolishly. He put the light out
before he opened the door.

'Who is it?' he said. 'Who's there?' It was, of course, a woman.
No man would have knocked so quietly, with the certainty that
this very quietness would carry its own insistence. 'Is anything
the matter?' he asked.

'Yes; I've killed him,' she answered. It was like a film, he
thought. It was only on the films that one got these startling
answers to ordinary, civilized questions. Even the theatre had
given up the shock tactics of melodrama, and in life – 'real life'
as some call it – they could not, surely, have a place, except,
perhaps, as incidents in a war.

He stepped up into the well at the tub's square stern, and
then down on to the stones.

'You don't mean you've murdered somebody?' he said, a
humorous note in his voice. She turned, so that the moonlight
showed her pale face and made her disordered hair a nimbus
about her head. She might have been a ghost, he thought, a
visitant from a shadowy borderland, with her light, thin dress
and the effect of unreality produced by the traitor moonlight.

'No,' she said nervously, as though she did not expect him to
believe her. 'He – he fell. That's what I shall say.'

Harben looked at her doubtfully. He could see that she was
terribly afraid. There was something she was keeping back. He

wanted to know what it was. He said briefly, 'Better come into the cabin and tell me all about it.'

The tub was deep in the ooze. It took a full tide to float it because it was drawn up so high. It inclined at an angle for which he himself made habitual, unconscious compensation whenever he stepped aboard, but it was not so easy for the girl. He gave her his hand, and by the time he had shut the door, relighted the lamp and turned round to look, she was leaning against the end of the bunk on which he himself had been seated.

Then he saw that it was not altogether the awkward slant of the floor which accounted for her attitude. She was not braced against the bunk, but had slithered and slumped herself on to it. He saw in her face the signs of an exhaustion so complete that the spirit could no longer force the body to its will. He said:

'You'd better lie down.'

There were two berths. The one on which she was supported he used as a seat for meals and when he was writing; the other was his bed. He stepped across the yard of space between himself and the girl, and lifted her on to his bunk.

'And now, what is it?' he said. 'Isn't it a doctor you want? – for him, I mean?'

'There's nothing to be done,' she answered. 'And I don't really care. He's dead. There's nothing to be done.'

'Well, tell me what happened,' said Harben. 'Were you alone in the house?'

'The others have gone,' she answered. 'And he – well, he just tumbled over the stool. I heard the thud, and I got there as soon as I could, but I couldn't even lift him on to his bed.'

'But if it was only an accident, what made you say you had killed him?'

'I left the stool there – I must have done – when I did the room this morning.'

'Well, that couldn't be helped. No one could blame you for that. Look, let's go back there together, as soon as you feel you can, and see what's doing, shall we?'

'No,' she said. 'No, I can't. I can't go in there again.'

'Well, give me the key, then, and I'll go.'

He did not know why he said this. The words were spoken

39

before he had fully realized what he was going to suggest. The girl's reaction was curious.

'I knew you would,' she said. He was going to argue that she could not have known anything of the sort, but a glance at her white face, shadowed eyes and the childishness of her relaxed, thin body warned him that it would be wiser not to argue.

'The key,' he said. 'I can't get in otherwise, can I?'

'No,' she answered, 'you can't. She half sat up and fumbled for it. The fingers he touched were cold as he took it from her.

'Don't worry,' he said. 'I'll be back as soon as I can.' He turned towards the door, but she clutched his sleeve.

'Put out the light,' she said.

'Can you see in the dark?' he asked, standing still and putting one hand on the bulkhead to keep his balance on the slant of the sloping floor.

'Enough for this,' she answered; and, drawing him to her, she took his head between long, thin hands and kissed him. The moonlight, washed on the tide to the sickle-shaped margin of land, etched blandly the hulks of the hoppers, the spars of the yacht, the roofs of the old men's houses, the willows, the hollows, the black and silver reeds.

A star blinked, reflecting a mood. Somewhere a dog howled. The river slid by without a sound, and, over the land and the water, the night, with its endless gyrations, danced and swam.

## CHAPTER FIVE

### *Satyr*

It was more than an hour after this that Harben crossed the streaked river bed and climbed the steps of the bank. The house was the third one along, a white-painted Georgian building, flat-fronted except for its porch. This was upheld on two pillars, and sheltered a broad-panelled door. The lock was smooth-working, and he entered the house with no sound except for the ominous one of the great door closing behind him.

Once he had begun to mount the stairs, the extraordinary and uncomfortable nature of his adventure came upon him with force, and he wondered what, in the first place, had compelled him to embark on it. The crazy hour which had passed had committed him irrevocably, however – or so he thought. He mounted three flights to the attics, and came at last to a carpetless, creaking landing on which one door stood open, showing a yellowish light.

He hesitated a second, and then went in. The contrast between the electric lighting of the staircase and the little candle burning in the attic was extraordinarily disquieting. It was fitting, however, he supposed, that a candle should illumine the house of death. He closed the door behind him and remained with his back against it to take his first survey of the room.

It was as the girl had described it – a large room, as attics go, with a sloping roof, a small, square window and a skylight on to the slates. It contained a single bed. The moonlight showed the bed clearly, and the candle, burnt to within two inches of its socket, showed the old man's body on the floor.

Harben was attacked by the same sense of unreality as that with which he had been assailed when the girl had answered his first question. He took up the candle and knelt at the old man's side.

He was lying on his back with his eyes open, and the stool over which he must have fallen had been placed against the wall near his head. His dressing-gown was in grotesque and heavy patterns of gold and green, and beneath it long pyjamas, striped white and purple, almost covered his feet. One slipper was on; the other had fallen off when he stumbled over the stool.

There was nothing Harben could do. He took a quilt from the bed and covered the old man with it, glanced round the shadowy room whose corners were equally blind to the glimmering candle and the moonlight flooding the bed, blew out the light and went down into the hall, switching off the lights as he descended.

He had seen the telephone, and went across to it, but, even as his hand went out, he changed his mind, and decided to wait until the morning. A few hours could make no difference, and the coward within him argued that by morning he might be able to take himself out of the business and leave it to those whom it concerned.

Following some subconscious line of thought, he tried the front door to make certain that it was fastened, and then went again to the attic. He lighted the stub of candle which still remained, then blew it out again, and went to the room below. He switched on the light and looked about the room. In contrast to the attic it was handsomely furnished with a large bed in walnut, matched by wardrobe, dressing-table and washstand. An armchair and a couple of small chairs stood on a beautiful carpet, and on a side-table was a radio-gramophone. A heavy walking-stick in one corner, a man's hair-brushes and collar-box on the dressing-table, a complete set of dentures in a tooth-glass on the washstand, and several pairs of men's boots and shoes in a neat row on a set of low shelves by the bed-head, gave complete confirmation to Harben's own certainty that the old man had chosen his own room in which to meet his death.

He went up the stairs again, heaved up the body from the landing, carried it down to the room to which, by inference, it belonged, and laid it with careful reverence on the bed. He arranged the ornate, expensive dressing-gown to fall in straight lines and dignified, sculptured folds.

The old man's eyes were staring open. Harben closed them. The mouth was open, too, but with that he did not interfere. It was discomforting to see that toothless, astonished maw; pathetic, too; not dreadful. It expressed the man's last thought – his surprise and horror at his fall; not the impulse which had taken him, as just on midnight, into another person's room. We die as we have lived, thought Harben, in spite of death-bed repentances and all the last rites of the Church.

Old satyr! – yet the dignity of the body, in the long, gold-glittering robe, was strangely pleasing. Harben covered the face, and, with this discreetly hooded, it was a king who lay there, straight and wonderfully silent, on his bier.

There was a sudden scratching and scrabbling from the heavy dark curtains at the window. Startled, Harben looked up. A small monkey, with a wizened, sad little face, and a parrot of brilliant plumage, both of them clinging to the curtain-pole, were, heads cocked shrewdly, gazing down on him.

## CHAPTER SIX

## *Mermaid*

The tide was coming in. There was already water between the tub and the bank. By morning the tub would be afloat.

Harben stepped over the foot and a half of shallow water between her stern and the shore, and opened the door to the cabin. He heard the girl move before he lighted the lamp, but he trimmed it carefully before he turned to look at her. Then he sat down and filled his pipe before he spoke.

'Yes, he was dead. We must call the doctor in the morning. And now, you'd better tell me what really happened, hadn't you?' he said.

'You know what happened. You saw he was in the wrong room. You know what I told you before.'

Harben struck a match and looked at her over it before he lighted his pipe. But he did not say any more. When his pipe was drawing, he rigged up a screen to shield the light from her eyes, sat down at the cabin table and drew his manuscript towards him. But the mood was gone. He altered a word or two here, and the turn of a sentence there, but at four o'clock he took off his shoes, unhitched a heavy waterproof from its nail and drew it over him as he stretched himself out on the bunk he had been using as a seat.

When he woke he had forgotten the unusual events of the night, and realized only that he was on the wrong side of the cabin. Then he remembered the girl, and leaned up on his elbow to look at her. She was not there, but the blankets were tumbled on the berth and the pillow showed a slight hollow.

Harben got up and filled his kettle from the jar of fresh water in the stern, put the kettle on to boil over a tiny spirit lamp, and then dropped his clothes on the floor and went for his morning swim.

The tub, not yet quite lifted by the tide, was now ten yards from land, and a pebbled beach covered with driftwood and odds and ends, and less than a yard at its widest, was all that could be seen of the expanse of ooze and stones of the previous night.

Harben stepped overside with the caution born of experience, found footing on ooze and not stones, and waded out into the river.

He felt the mud settle and shift between his toes. Suddenly the bed shelved sharply. He was up to his armpits in water, for the centre channel was dredged. He began to swim very fast, for the water was cold. Dark-brown, it swirled and rolled. Harben ducked under and swam with it, frisking like a porpoise to get warm.

The river sucked and streamed, as though it, and not the man, were alive. Harben came to the surface, his head as sleek as a seal's, his shoulders and chest, his tingling arms and legs, countering the impact of the water.

Downstream there was an island, a narrow, willow-bordered eyot. He swam to it, and climbed out on to the bank. As he landed, he heard a splash from the opposite side, which was hidden from him by the willows. Another swimmer, he thought. A number of boys and men were accustomed to bathe from the foreshore at about that time in the morning.

He took no further heed, but, looking across at the opposite bank of the river, he noticed that the Georgian house was facing him, forcing him to consider the fantastic events of the night. It occurred to him that it would have simplified matters, after all, to have called up a doctor from the house instead of waiting these hours until the morning. It even came into his head that occasions of violent (even if of accidental) death, were, properly, the business of the police.

These first stirrings of discomfort and regret began to nag at him. He blamed himself for not having reported the death as soon as he had known it had occurred. If everything came out, there would be the devil to pay.

The swimmer came round the long spit of mud at the eastern end of the island, and he saw that it was the girl. She swam with ease and great power, and the river, quiet at full tide, curved past her side like the curving wave past a ship.

Harben pushed back among the willows, content to watch her. The thin green leaves of the willows touched his hair and moved restlessly over his shoulders. The rough ground pricked his hams and the backs of his thighs. Coarse grass thrust between his toes and against his legs, and his heels were sunk in the ooze.

When he lost sight of the girl behind the piers of the bridge, he slipped into the water again and began to swim, with a long, strong stroke, easily and lazily after her; but had not gone half-way towards the bridge when she saw her returning. She did not slacken speed, but swam as fish swim, unheeding, and as though her body were merely heavier and more opaque than the element which supported and confirmed it. She was a part of that element, and more than native to it. It was as though she and the water were the same thing differently expressed by an artist whose creative power was limitless, thought Harben, and all of whose creatures had the perfection of immortality.

Harben turned again and swam after the girl. He thought she had not seen him, but, after a moment, she also turned (he could have sworn he caught the flash of a fish's tail) and they swam side by side towards the boat.

'I'd like to swim out to sea,' she suddenly said.

'We're going that way,' said Harben. She laughed, and the face she turned towards him was young and fresh, pink as the inside of a sea-shell, and with all the weariness and childish distress of the nightfall washed out of it as though the river had magic, to take away suffering and evil.

When they came to the boat she climbed aboard. Harben swam past, but she leaned out over the side and clutched his thick, boyish hair. Pain made him stop. He laughed.

'Come aboard. You're cold,' she said. She released him, and he clambered over the stern and picked up a bucket for water to rinse his muddy feet. Then he put down the bucket and pushed her towards the cabin. She resisted the pressure on her shoulder, and turned towards him. They held each other's eyes as

antagonists will before a fight, and then she pulled him inside.
They left the door swinging, dried themselves with anticipatory
haste, knocked elbow against elbow, laughed, drew sharp, short
breath, as though they had been running very fast.

Their bodies were cold from the river, and then, with frightening suddenness, surgingly warm, except for cold fingers
clutching at shoulder and waist, and a cold mouth pressed on
the living warmth of the flesh. Lean belly and rounded thigh,
the pressure of deltoid and heel, strong shoulder and urgent
hand, lost shape and meaning. Agony passed like a sword, effort
broke out in sweat, and stars stood, shivered and swam.

Harben recovered soonest. He pushed the wet hair from his
eyes, got off the bunk, picked up his shirt, and said sadly:

'Well, that's that. And now what the devil do we do?'

## CHAPTER SEVEN

## *Fugitive*

The girl finished combing her hair. Without looking at Harben
she went to the stern of the tub and blocked the doorway with
her body. Harben, after a pause, went out to her and stood
behind her, putting his hands on her arms.

'Come on,' he said. 'It's got to be done, I'm afraid. Do you
very much mind going back?'

'No,' she answered, 'of course not.' Her eyes were still gazing
at the river as it endlessly, endlessly flowed. For the river there
was no going back; not even the flood tide could take the stream
back to its beginnings. Such were her nebulous thoughts, but
she did not word them; she did not think in words, as Harben
did.

'Come along,' he said, 'we've got to report it, you know.
You're not to blame, and nothing can harm him now.'

They had to use the dinghy, which they beached on the small
spit of gravel and mud which the outgoing tide had left at the
foot of the steps.

They met no one between the top of the steps and the house they sought, except for a couple of old men from the almshouses enjoying a stroll in the sunshine. There were men in the boat-builder's yard, and men in the slip, but they did not see them, although they could hear them working. Harben greeted the two old men, but they did not seem to recognize the girl.

The girl had the key of the house. Harben had remembered to return it. She unlocked the fine, broad door and pushed it open. Then she stood back and let Harben go in first. He went to the foot of the stairs, then turned and said:

'Coming up? We'd better see him first, you know.'

'Aren't you going to telephone?' she asked.

'Yes, if you like. I just thought – ' He went back to where she stood on the step and, taking her hand, drew her in. But she refused to go even as far as the foot of the staircase.

'Aren't you coming?' he asked.

'To see him? No. I will wait for you. Please don't be long. And don't shut the front door. I want it open. I want to be able to run.'

He looked at her, but said nothing. He was not long. In fact, he came down again immediately, the news in his face before he spoke.

'He's gone!' he said. 'He isn't there any more.'

'Gone? Gone from the attic?' Her green eyes were clear as glass, and as expressionless.

'I carried him – I thought he'd be better in his own room. At least, I supposed it was his room. The room directly underneath. I – you wouldn't care to come up? In fact, you've got to come up.' He shut the front door with a bang and turned to face her.

She made no protest, and, this time, showed no fear and no reluctance. She followed him up the stairs without a word. He noticed that her footfalls made no sound. He looked round twice; but she was there, very pale, green-haired and ghost-like, just behind his shoulder.

Harben looked into the room, but still the great bed was empty. The counterpane was smooth and showed no crease, the pillows were plumped up as though the old man's head had not been placed there. The curtains were all drawn back and the room was sunny. The light shone on the sombre walls of the room, but not on the golden patterns of the old man's splendid gown.

'I laid him on the bed,' said Harben. The girl had come up beside him. And had placed a long hand on his arm. 'I laid him there on the bed and covered his face.'

'What with?' The question seemed banal and inappropriate, and he glanced at her sharply as he answered.

'My handkerchief. I had a silk handkerchief in my pocket.'

'You don't think – ' She studied his face. 'You don't think you left him in the attic? You don't think you *dreamt* you moved him?'

'I *know* I carried him down here. There was a monkey up on the curtain pole, and a parrot.'

'Then what are we going to do? It must mean that someone has been here, and – there wasn't anyone to come! And why don't you call me Leda? You sound so cold and unkind!'

'But *why* should anyone come here? And why should they move him? I'm going up to the attic!' said Harben brusquely.

And up he went, leaving her on the landing. He opened the attic door, but the body was not to be seen. He went to the window and looked out on to the river. Then he explored the adjoining rooms. They were musty, but not more so than most disused rooms of their kind. One of them overlooked the lush, untidy garden, and he noted a giant laburnum, which trailed incredible inflorescences like arrested cascades of gold, almost on to the ground.

He returned to the first attic, looked out of the window, and pondered on something that was wrong; not wildly, nightmare-ishly wrong, like the dead man's disappearance and the tidying-up of the room, but mundanely, ordinarily wrong, some small thing out of focus. He could not call anything to mind, shouted cheerfully over the banisters to the girl, then came down the stairs and went again into the bedroom. He felt like a squirrel in a cage. Something was certainly amiss.

He went to the window and looked out. His eyes roved up and down the river. The girl was no longer in the room. She must have gone downstairs again; and, what was more, the dinghy was no longer at the foot of the steps, and the tub was no longer at her moorings. That was what had been wrong with the view from the attic window. He had seen it without realizing what he had noticed; his mind had been so crowded with strange thoughts that the obvious had not immediately impinged upon his consciousness.

Curiously enough, he did not at once connect the disappearance of his property with the girl. It was some time later that he discovered that she had gone. He had made another discovery. The old man had been terribly sick before his death. Harben, accustomed to seasick passengers – for the tub was a sea-going craft – cleaned up the vomit methodically, and then left the house.

He ran downstairs, pulled open the great front door and peered cautiously out. Two women went past. He waited, then peered out again. A boat, ferried quickly and skilfully with one oar over the stern was paddled into the mud-beach by a waterman's boy, who jumped ashore and came whistling up the steps and turned into his grandfather's yard. Harben knew him well, and waited until he had gone.

After that, there was no one. Harben shut the door, walked quickly to the nearest narrow alley, ran down it with long strides, dropped into a walk at the end, gained a side-street, and walked along it, and came out at the foot of the bridge.

A friend of his had a boat there, kept at private moorings in a dirty little backwater on the Middlesex side of the river.

The friend was not on the boat, so Harben borrowed it. But there was no sign of the tub, and he found himself in a dilemma, for the girl might have gone downstream towards London just as easily as up-river. There was nothing to guide him in his search.

He went up-river as far as Windsor, and there, at moorings just off Clewer, settled down for the night. He could not sleep, and had not even his manuscript to console him. He thought continually and unprofitably of the girl and his odd adventure. He got up as soon as it was dawn, and decided to go for a swim. The sun was not up, but in the grey-gold morning he could see a pennon fluttering at the stern. He dropped his towel and put out a hand to touch the pennon, for it was his own. At least, he thought so at first. Then he discovered that it was like his, but a new one. A piece of paper was pinned to the gay little triangle of silk. He fingered the pennon curiously before he took out the pins. Where had she got it? he wondered.

Naked and shivering, he carried the paper back with him into the cabin, sat down on his bunk and pulled the blankets round him, and, by the glow of the cabin lamp, which he had left burning because the cabin portholes were too small to let in the feeble light of the dawn, he read the note.

'I love you too much to get you into trouble. The tub is by the lock near the Great Park. Finish your book. I shall read it. Good-bye. I shall pray for you. Leda.'

Harben turned it over. There was no more. He went on deck again, tore the message across, and dropped the pieces in the river. The river sang softly here in the upper reaches. Mechanically, he tied his towel about him, leaned over the side and craned his head to watch the paper dancing downstream.

People from other moorings began to clatter plates, preparing breakfast. Voices and laughter came across the water. The trees of the island swayed, and rustled their leaves. The river slipped quietly by, as green and dark as the dreams with which poets have so often compared it.

Harben put a hand on the gunwhale and neatly jumped over the stern. His down-dropping feet touched weed. He kicked himself up to the surface, and, swimming his strongest, rounded the bend of the backwater out to where the main stream, flashing grey-silver in the sun, and running in sullen green beneath the banks, wound like a serpent from Windsor to Boveney Lock.

The current was strong. He breasted it, swimming madly until his arms ached. Then he swam round to the backwater, loose-muscled and tired. The water was calm at the moorings; he could see the dark hull of the boat like a wavering snake. Then he lifted his head, and her outline was firmly before him.

People were up and about, and the backwater rang with their voices. He tried to imagine that Leda would bend towards him over the gunwhale, her damp hair dark with the water, its gold and its green all gone, her witch's mouth smiling, her green eyes alight with laughter. He tried to believe she would catch him again by the hair, and draw him into the cabin.

But no one was aboard. The well and the cabin seemed dead. He dried himself slowly, had breakfast, and then went ashore at Clewer and walked back through Windsor town and out again along the towing path. The lock was upstream beyond Eton.

The lock-keeper said he knew nothing of any lady. The boat-builder's men had found the tub among their rowing-boats, punts and canoes, and were anxious to have it moved. Harben took over his property and recompensed them for their trouble. The tank was almost empty, and a little of the food had been used; otherwise all was exactly as he had left it. He searched in vain for anything Leda had left – a message; even a handkerchief. There was nothing; not even a few stray hairs from that baffling green-gold head. But the old pennon was still on his boat. He put the new one tenderly into the flag-locker.

He watched the papers for weeks, but there was no reference to the death of the old man. The house by the river, and the death which had occurred in it, might both have been the figments of a dream. He returned his friend's motor-boat, returned for the tub, and, in spite of an instinct of danger, went back to the house by the river and took up his moorings again.

For weeks he looked out for the police. For weeks he looked in the agony columns of the newspapers for another message from Leda. All day, and for hours after dark and at early morning, he watched the house. He saw nothing, but could not believe that nothing was happening there; for he had the impression that there were comings and goings, although who came and went, and why, he could not discover. One day it would be a chance remark made by his friend the boat-builder or by one of the boat-builder's men; sometimes a woman from one of the barges had some sing-song word about lights of various colours in a house ashore which misled the tug-boats into thinking they had got to the bridge; sometimes it was his own instinct which told him that the house was not always uninhabited.

In spite of his anxieties his book made progress. He ceased, by the end of July, to watch the agony columns in the news-papers. The newspapers, in fact, had become disquieting, not from the point of view of his narrow field, but upon wider issues. War stalked near. At last September came.

## CHAPTER EIGHT

## *Nuns*

When war broke out the tub was lying far upriver, beside the main road to the little riverside town of Helsey Marsh.

Harben had been there for three days before the Sunday on which the first air-raid alarm sounded thrillingly but abortively over London. He had brought the tub upstream to accommodate that same friend whose boat he had borrowed to follow Leda, but the friend had been called away at the last moment, and Harben had made the lazy man's decision to stay where he was rather than bother to go downstream again to his old moorings. In any case, the tub would be laid up soon, he had reflected, particularly if the autumn turned suddenly cold.

He rose at six on the morning war was declared, and was in the water before the mist had cleared. He seemed to be swimming as much in the mist as in the river. All the green banks and the heavy green of the trees seemed to swim in the water with him. He might have been under the water instead of in it. It was a baffling, beautiful, exquisitely strange experience. He remembered no morning quite like it. He had had his third dream of Leda, and, as he swam, he half-expected to meet her swimming towards him out of the green mist, her green hair part of it.

The water was bitterly cold; colder than he remembered it even in the days of early spring when the willow-catkins were mystical pointers to Easter and the lesser celandine was still in bud on the banks.

He struck out into the middle of the stream until he could see neither shore. Then he swam fast, and felt warmth tingling back to his shoulders and flowing back into his loins. His hands and feet remained cold. Suddenly the green of the water grew deeper and thicker, and his fingers, reaching downward, felt the slime of the sloping bank. He swung out a little, kept parallel with the bank, and then began to cross the stream again.

Suddenly, when, as he judged, he was near enough to the middle of the stream, he heard a motor boat approaching. How far off it was he found himself unable to tell. He raised himself in the water, and shouted, at the top of his lungs:

'Ahoy there! Swimmer! Look out!' Then he listened, and, to his relief, the motor boat shut off her engine. There was no other response to his hail, so he swam for the bank; but, before he could reach it, a rowing-boat loomed up beside him. A voice said:

'Now!' And a boat-hook chopped down almost on top of his head. Harben duck-dived away, then, turning, swam under the boat and came up on the opposite side. Immediately it was swallowed up in the mist. Soundlessly paddling with his hands, he propelled himself onwards, away from the point of peril, and got to the bank, but not the bank by which the tub was moored. He dared not get out of the water. He deduced that there were at least two men in the boat, and he felt that the odds of two men armed with boat-hook and oars against himself, naked and defenceless, were likely to prove too long.

Submerged to the nostrils, he held by a little bush and waited. He heard the sound of their oars, but could not see anything but the thick mist over the water and the dark little shrub to which he clung. Then the sound of the oars died away.

He listened and waited, and strained his eyes. The cold of the water began to seep into his bones. It petrified his muscles and then his mind. He could not feel his feet, and the hand that clutched the bush seemed frozen stiffly to the branches. At last he heard the motor boat engine again, and was not surprised to hear the sounds die away.

Even then he did not stir, and it was well for him that he did not, for, after another few minutes, during which he wondered whether he would ever be able to force his petrified limbs to propel him across the river and down to the tub, he heard the boatmen coming back. They actually let their craft drift near him by the bank, at which they were slashing with the oars and cursing when the clumsy dinghy grounded and they had to stop to shove her off again. But they missed him this time by a yard or two, and one of them was cursing as they went by. The other voice argued that they had certainly killed him.

As soon as the dinghy had disappeared in the mist, Harben thrust off quietly from the bank, submerged himself within a yard of the bush to which he had been clinging, and, head under water and swimming a slow, strong breast stroke to keep himself down, he made for the opposite shore.

He came up to breathe, reached forward, and found his hands in the roots of a tree. At this he turned cautiously, and kept under the bank, where the river, on that side, was deep, and swam back to the tub.

He was unable to hold his towel when he got out, so regardless of water dripping quickly on to the floor, he dried and dressed in the cabin. Even as he pushed the door open, his heart jumped, half-expecting somebody there. But the cabin was empty. Among his kit of tools he had a hammer. He placed it in a handy position.

The morning passed with its slow beauty. The mist cleared away about nine, and he sat in the well and smoked and pondered until twelve. Then he got out his manuscript and devoted himself to his book.

He had no wireless set, and did not hear the declaration of war, but at just after two in the afternoon he was surprised and amused to see small processions of children, all carrying bags and bundles, walking along the lane which led from the main road into the sleepy little town.

He did not immediately relate the sight of these children to the heavy tidings of war, but thought, at first, that several Sunday schools had decided to hold their summer outings on the same day. Then it occurred to him that Sunday schools did not, as a general rule, hold their annual treats on a Sunday, and he began to wonder, idly, what explanation there could be.

He analysed the impression which had given rise to the idea of Sunday school treats – for he was accustomed to amuse himself with this sort of semi-silly introspection – and came to the conclusion that it was the sight of two nuns which had engendered the theory in his mind.

These nuns were not, of course, the only adults in charge of the parties of children, but, whereas the other parties only passed by once, these nuns and their little group of boys must have gone by half a dozen times.

Each time the party went by it seemed to have become a little smaller. He began to count the children, and, by four in the afternoon, their number had dropped from seventeen down to five.

As they came to a stretch of short grass very close to the tub, one of the nuns, an elderly woman, grey in the face with fatigue, told the boys to sit down. They had taken rest several times before, but not close to where Harben was seated. The nuns themselves remained standing, their hands folded neatly away in the wide white sleeves of their habits. They were, he guessed, Dominicans.

There was nowhere to sit, except on the grass itself. Harben, his chivalry provoked by the sight of the patient women, went ashore, approached them, bowed and said:

'Good afternoon. Won't you come and sit in my boat?'

He did not remember having spoken to nuns before. These smiled, and the older one answered gravely and graciously:

'Thank you. You are kind.'

He handed them on board. The older nun was heavy and, although she disguised it, nervous of taking the step between the shore and the boat. Harben held her hand firmly, and, as naturally as his mother might have done, she clasped his strong fingers and let him support and direct her.

The younger nun was not much more than a girl. Her eyes were the colour of harebells, and she took the long stride as though she had lived on boats for the whole of her life. They would not enter the cabin, but seated themselves, very upright and soldierly, in the well. Suddenly the older nun gave a slight moan and pitched forward.

Her head struck the door of the cabin. She fell in, and lay stretched in the narrow space between the narrow berths, completely blocking the entrance.

Harben, moving carefully, bestrode the prostrate woman, took
her under the armpits and heaved her upwards. There was not
sufficient room to bring her, unconscious as she was and a dead
weight on his arms, completely clear of the cabin, and the young
nun could not get inside to help him, but he managed to get the
sick nun to one of the bunks. He covered her with a rug and
came out again to her young and lovely companion.

'She'll be all right in there,' he said. 'We must just let her rest
for a bit.' The young nun, entering the cabin, knelt down and
began to chafe her companion's hands.

'Do you think you can manage? Call if you want me, please.
I'll be just outside. I shall hear you,' Harben said.

'You are so good,' she answered. He pointed to the water-jar.

'That's fresh. My tooth-glass is the only tumbler, I'm afraid,
but it's perfectly clean.'

He went back to the well of the boat. One or two of the boys
had come up.

'Hungry?' asked Harben. They shook their heads.

'We've had plenty to eat,' said the biggest boy. 'Only, we've
no place to sleep.'

'They evacuated us this morning. We're orphans,' volunteered
another. 'We've come from London.'

Light dawned on Harben. Part, at any rate, of his curiosity
was satisfied.

'Oh, I see,' he said. 'Aren't there supposed to be billets?'

'No one will have us,' said the boy. 'They see the sisters, and
they think we want charity. But the Government pays for us just
like anybody else. The sisters say so. They tell the people. Some
of them took the little 'uns, but no one will bother with us. The
Government *do* pay, don't they, sir?'

'Sure,' said Harben, who knew nothing whatever about it.
'Sure they do. Why not? Which convent orphanage do you come
from?'

'It's called St Vincent's Hospice, attached to the Dominican
Convent,' said the boy. 'It's in Soho, near Drury Lane.'

'What are the nuns called?'

'The Third Order of Preachers, Dominicans.'

'No. I mean – their own names.'

'Nuns don't use their own names,' said the second boy. 'The old one is Sister Mary Sebastian, and the young one is Sister Mary Dominic. *She* is really a nurse, but Sister Mary James the Less had to have all her teeth out yesterday, so, of course, she couldn't come.'

'I see,' said Harben. 'So you all want somewhere to sleep? We must see what we can do.'

As he uttered these rash words, Sister Mary Dominic came out of the cabin and smiled at him. Harben made room for her beside him, and she seated herself composedly, so that they were at an angle to one another, he on the starboard locker and she in the stern-sheets.

'How is Sister Mary Sebastian?' he asked. She smiled again.

'How clever of you to know her name. I think she will do now, but I wish I knew where to lodge her for the night. And these poor boys. I do not know what will become of them.'

'You should have the faith that removes mountains,' said Harben gravely. Then he added seriously, 'If it comes to the worst we could bed the boys down on this boat. Or you and Sister Mary Sebastian could have it.'

'I must get something settled very soon,' she said, staring down at her white serge scapula so that all he could see were the long lashes resting on her cheek.

Harben stared down at his own brown hands which were dangling between his knees and then looked up and said:

'I'll settle it for you. Don't worry. I'll go into the village and pull it about their ears if they don't do what we want.'

'Will you?' she said, taking him at his word with the eagerness and simplicity of a child. 'You are so good. Will you not tell me your name?' He laughed, but, when he had told her his name, she said:

'You write books. I know the name.'

'Very bad books, I'm afraid. Do they read novels in convents?'

'No, not often. But I have not always been in a convent. I am afraid your books *are* very bad. Not bad in the sense you mean, but your ideas are false, like your modesty – false and wrong.'

'They are true to life,' said Harben, 'and life is a thing you know little about, I imagine.'

'They are not true to God.' She looked full at him. 'I must not tell you how much I hate your ideas because God has put it into your heart to show us kindness, and that means He loves you, and you, I think, love Him, and perhaps your books don't matter.'

'No,' said Harben, 'I don't love God. In fact, I don't believe in Him. There isn't any sense in it, you know.'

'Yes, oh yes, there is. Believe me, I do know that,' she answered gently. 'I will pray for you. You have so good a heart that you *must* love God, whether you know it or not.'

Harben laughed, and, to change the subject, said:

'Which houses have you tried? The biggest ones?'

'Oh, no!' she answered. 'Only the cottages! Rich people would not take our boys, I am afraid.'

'That's were I think you're wrong,' he answered. 'I must remark again upon your lack of faith.' He looked her straight in the face, and went off whistling. Down-river lay a quiet, sandy lane which ran parallel to the water. In this lane were a number of large, pretentious, comfortable sort of houses, each with a frontage to the river. Some were let for the summer, others were occupied by their owners. He did not know any of the people, so marched straight up to the first high wooden gate, walked up the gravel path and knocked at the door. No one seemed to be at home, so, after having knocked three times, he gave up, and tried the next house. This was called *The Island*. It had a bright red door picked out with mouldings of white, a brilliant door-knocker, a letter-box and scraper of brass which looked like gold, geraniums in ornamental pots on either side of the porch, and a general air of middle-class cheerfulness and comfort.

Rather to Harben's surprise, a manservant opened the door; a dark-haired, respectable fellow, probably over forty. He and Harben took one another in, and then Harben said, almost awkwardly:

'Do you think – can I see the owner of the house?'

'Why, yes, sir,' replied the man. 'What name, please, would it be?'

'Harben. David Harben. I represent a couple of Dominican nuns.'

'Please come in sir,' said the man, betraying no surprise at this announcement.

Harben entered a white-walled, blue-carpeted room, and was admiring a finely-carved desk when the servant returned, observed, with correct composure, 'This way, sir, if you please,' and led him to a dark-panelled dining-room which overlooked the river.

A small, ugly, curiously vital old lady, with sharp black eyes, a yellow skin and a grin like that of an anticipatory crocodile, beckoned him forward. A table on which was a silver tray of tea-things was standing beside her chair, but she had finished tea and seemed to have been reading, for a book lay open on the table bedside the tray. She was dressed in rose-colour. Her gown was unbecoming and not in the mode. Her hands were like claws, but her voice was deep and lovely. Harben bowed, with the sense that he must be in the presence of royalty, and remained at a discreet, respectful distance.

'I have heard of you, child,' said the old woman. 'Come to the fire. You're a novelist. Sit down. What's all this about nuns?'

Harben explained, and besought her to offer the boys her hospitality, if only for one night. He painted a lurid picture of an air-raid on London, particularly on the district from which the lads had come. Almost before he had finished, however, he realized that the description was unnecessary. The old lady grinned.

'Do you suppose that the boys have toothbrushes?' she demanded. 'The nuns, of course, chew bones. Go off and get them at once. Dominicans, you say? What's a war, if we can't have fun?'

Her laughter pursued him to the door. The manservant let him out. He ran back towards his boat like a boy with good news for his mother. A quarter of an hour later he was leading his flock up the road towards *The Island*. The procession had a strange, unlikely appearance. In the van came Harben, agent of God, supporting, as a courtier might a queen, the feeble steps of Sister Mary Sebastian. Following them came the boys; and in the rear of the company, walking alone, came Sister Mary Dominic.

At the garden gate stood the oddest of all God's agents, the old woman extremely like a witch who was to act as hostess to the party. On her thick black hair which showed not the slightest trace of grey she wore a chip straw hat Meg Merriles might have envied, and on her beaky little mouth was a crocodile grin which was intended as a smile of welcome. Harben presented the nuns to the witch as gracefully as he could without knowing the hostess's name. She supplied it with a cackle.

'My name is Lestrange Bradley.' She turned to the group of boys.

'Shoes off children, in the hall. These are not my carpets,' she said.

'You – can't accommodate *all* of us?' Sister Mary Dominic enquired with extraordinary timidity.

'Why not?' enquired Mrs Bradley. 'I've rented the house indefinitely, and probably shan't use it much myself.'

As though this were sufficient answer, she led the way in, motioned Harben to conduct the Dominicans to the dining-room, and herself stayed to supervise the boys.

'Do any of you children need hot-water bottles in your beds?' she asked in threatening tones.

'No, madam,' they replied in respectful chorus. Their hostess, hooting harshly, led them upstairs.

# BOOK THREE

## Enchantment

*

His hound is mute; his steed at will
Roams pastures deep with asphodel;
His queen is to her slumber gone;
His courtiers mute lie, hewn in
stone;
He hath forgot where he did hide
His sceptre in the mountain-side.

Walter de la Mare

---

### CHAPTER NINE

## *Sibyl*

Harben spent the night on the tub, but did not sleep. His adventure of the very early morning had caused him to provide himself with an efficient weapon in the form of a home-made sandbag, and he proposed to sit up and wait for the aggressors if they should have decided to make another attempt upon his life.

He did not altogether expect them, for he concluded that they hoped their object had been attained. It could be only a matter of time, however, before they came to the knowledge that he was still alive, unless he could find some way of concealing himself so that he could not be traced, and the chance of that was remote.

As he sat in his little cabin he thought about the mysterious affair in which he had involved himself, and then, idly at first, but later with a quickened interest, about Mrs Lestrange Bradley, the odd, shrewd, infinitely charitable hostess of the nuns and the orphan boys.

His brain worked slowly. It must have been three o'clock in the morning before he realized who she must be. He was almost tempted to place credence in Sister Mary Dominic's all-watchful Providence when the realization came to him, for Mrs Bradley was famous. She must be, he decided, the psychologist and detective who was one of the consultative experts called in by Scotland Yard when they had a baffling case or an interesting prisoner. She was, in short, the very person to consult about Leda, provided she could be sworn to secrecy, at any rate for a time.

The police would want to know all sorts of things which he did not want to disclose to them. He had placed himself, it was clear, in a very invidious position, so far as the law was concerned, by his neglect to report the finding of the body and, still more, by his decision to say nothing of its strange disappearance.

He was not the kind of person who would ever have thought of claiming police protection and yet he had scarcely enjoyed that river-washed man-hunt of the morning. In fact, if he were going in fear of his life, it would be most improbable (he thought, putting what, to him, were first things first) that he would be able to settle down and get on with his book, and that would be a nuisance.

To tell Mrs Bradley the truth, to request her for her advice, and, if it seemed reasonable, to take it, were tempting ideas. He spent the rest of the night in trying to resist them.

One thing he decided to do, although his masculinity revolted at first against it. Common sense prevailed, however, on this point, and at eight o'clock in the morning he went to *The Island* to ask Mrs Bradley if she needed help in coping with her guests. Her house would be a haven if she would have him.

'Why, yes,' she said, 'why not? Sister Mary Sebastian will need to rest for a time, and it is unfair to expect Sister Mary Dominic to undertake sole charge of the boys, I think. You had better go and talk to her about it. I've just chased her out of the sickroom. She's in the garden.'

Harben had seen her upon his walk up the path, but she had gone to the back of the house by the time he got out there again, and was standing by Mrs Bradley's little landing-stage near the boathouse, looking across the green river at the woods on the opposite side.

'Pleasanter here than in Soho,' said Harben, by way of greeting.'

'Indeed, yes. So green, so quiet, so kind,' she responded, lifting her eyes to his face and giving him her strangely heart-searching smile. Harben thought of the vicious attack which had been engineered against him on just this quiet water, and laughed at her, but agreed.

'Do you not really think so?' she enquired.

'No, I don't altogether think so,' he replied. 'I am in agreement with Sherlock Holmes, you know, about the country. Dark deeds can be committed more easily, and with less chance of being known, than in the streets and crowded tenements of a town.'

'But dark deeds happen in cities,' she responded. 'There was murder in Soho, not so long ago.'

'Yes. Soho is dark and deep, like parts of this weedy river,' he agreed. 'I live there all the winter, and ought to know. I suppose it's the foreign element. I know we've had knife fights, and that sort of thing, in our neighbourhood, and one is always coming up against what one might call the elements of vice. It's a very interesting neighbourhood for a writer.'

'And for our convent,' she said. 'Indeed, I think our convents should always be in the dark places of the earth. We are called the Third Order of Preachers, and, like Our Blessed Lord, should prefer sinners to the congregation of the righteous, for, to them, we can do most good.'

'And those boys,' said Harben, a good deal more interested in sociology than in what he privately termed 'religious bunk', and influenced, in any case, far more by Sister Mary Dominic's beauty than by her apologetics, 'what sort of homes do they come from?'

'From all kinds, and not, by any means, all from the Soho district,' she responded; and proceeded to give him details and statistics.

'You mean, then, that many of those boys are potential criminals,' he suggested, when she had finished.

'I prefer to think of them as the children of light,' she responded. 'There is just as much opportunity for them to be good as to be evil, and much more encouragement, I believe. It is true that we are born in sin, but goodness is stronger than evil. If I did not know that to be truth, I should not be where I am.'

'I can't understand that,' he said. 'What *does* make women take to the cloister?'

'I am not cloistered,' she said gently. 'We derive from the friars, not the monasteries. We do not live out of the world, but tremendously, gloriously in it. We have our teachers and nurses, our social settlements, our missionaries.' She smiled at him again. 'We are even regarded as heretics, you know, by some of the Catholic orders.'

'But you keep the monastic vows,' persisted Harben. 'You are celibate, poor, and obedient to superiors, are you not?'

'How else could we live and do our work?'

'You should not have chosen celibacy,' he said gently. 'Surely marriage and children are to be preferred, especially by women, to loneliness, barrenness and the rather uninteresting ideology you practise?'

'It depends on the point of view,' she answered quietly. 'Are you married, Mr Harben?'

'No. I have work to do. But – does this shock you? – I take my pleasure when I can get it.'

'It does not shock me. It seems to me grievously wrong.'

'I don't see that.'

'Have you never harmed anybody by it? That seems to me the first test.'

'I have not harmed the women. Doesn't that let me out? They enjoyed it as much as I did.'

'I cannot discuss it,' she said; and went indoors. Later, she said to Mrs Bradley, 'You do not talk to me.'

'You are a soldier,' said Mrs Bradley. 'So am I. We are under authority, both of us.'

'You mean the authority of God?'

'I mean the authority of *noblesse oblige*, child, a far more powerful conception, it seems to me.'

'You are wrong,' said the young nun, studying the ugly, intellectual, lively face of her hostess, 'but you are good. I know that. And I interrupted you. Please forgive me.'

'No, no!' said Mrs Bradley, to this apology. 'What do you make of Mr Harben?'

'I think he is in some trouble. I think he has done something wrong.'

'You are a very acute psychologist.'

'No, but I like him,' said Sister Mary Dominic, troubled. 'I wish he were a Catholic. I think Confession would help him.'

'It *will* help him,' said Mrs Bradley, absently. 'He shall confess to me.'

She did not need to look up to be able to visualize the consternation on Sister Mary Dominic's lovely brow, but as she took out her knitting, the corners of her beaked lips slightly twitched, as though she found something humorous in the silence.

Next day she called on Harben to accompany her round the garden whilst she snipped off dead flowers. He, already fond of her astringent and lively society, was nothing loth, and for a time they snipped busily and collected the snippings with tidy and efficient care. Then she said, straightening up:

'Let's go and sit down. I must get the crick out of my back. I suppose you never get a crick in yours?'

'Don't I, though?' said Harben. They seated themselves in the loggia, and Mrs Bradley drew off her gardening gloves.

'Well, who is she?' she said. 'And how did you come to lose her?'

Harben, as well he might, looked completely astonished at this. Then he caught her eye and smiled gravely:

'Touché, madame,' he said. 'What do you want to know? And am I being psycho-analysed?'

'Please yourself about that,' she answered. Then she waited, her black eyes no longer on him, but on the vista before her, the lawn in terraces and levels, the flower-beds burning towards autumn, the flashing river with the massed dark trees on its farther side, where the ground rose steeply from the banks and the faint ethereal blue of September skies lit the long flight of birds already in line for the south.

'You see,' said Harben, 'it's rather a queer story . . .'

It took him about a quarter of an hour to tell it all. He included the attack on him on the fourth of September.

'What do you think?' he added. Mrs Bradley got up.

'I'd like to see that other house by the river. I'd like a change. I'd like to be in London again. I've promised to visit a hospital in Soho. I ought to get back to my house in Kensington,' she said. She led him towards the back door, and on the way they deposited the gardening tools in the shed.

'But what do you make of it?' asked Harben. It had not struck him, until he had to put it into words which would be comprehensible to a critical and disinterested third party, what an extraordinary story it was which he had to tell.

'All sorts of things,' said Mrs Bradley. 'A mysterious night visitor, a corpse, a vanishing lady, a murderous attack at dawn from unknown men – you would reject these items both separately and *in toto*, I presume, if you were offered them as ingredients of a plot for one of your books?'

'Yes,' He did not qualify this unconditional admission.

'Yes,' she repeated thoughtfully. 'And yet they say that art is as large as life. It is, at any rate, twice as natural. And, of course, we shall find, shall we not, that they are men you know well?'

'You think I have told you an unnatural tale? In short, you don't believe me?'

'Why should I not believe you? Have you advertised for the girl?'

'It wouldn't be any good. Besides, whatever happens, I mustn't put the police on her track.'

'And yet, to solve your mystery, we must get in touch with her. Will you object if *I* advertise for her? I promise to be discreet.'

'I'd do anything . . .' he hesitated.

'To solve the mystery of what happened to the old man's body?'

'No. Just to see her again.'

'You realize that, on your own statement, she may be a murderess, don't you?'

'He fell, you know. And she couldn't have moved the body.'

'We have nothing but her word for the first of those statements, and your deductions for the second.'

'I see that. But I've met her.'

'Claudius met Messalina,' said Mrs Bradley. 'I am not making any challenging comparisons, but I do state facts.'

'I had hoped you would help me,' said Harben, 'but I can't agree that Leda killed the old man, except by way of accident, and I believe the accident happened as she described it.'

'Yes, but, speaking of facts, let us consider dispassionately, child, without prejudice, exactly those which you have given me. From out of the night a girl comes to your boat. Why does she select yours, and not somebody else's? Why choose to come to a yachtsman at all? Surely she had neighbours along the river front? I say nothing about her having chosen a man, rather than a woman, as her confidante. Women, especially young women, are apt to confide in men. Men quite often confide in women, too. It is understandable. Each sex expects to be able to hoodwink the other, to some extent, and as very few of our doings in this life will bear (in our own opinion) the full light of day, the instinct is probably a sound one, as instincts go. But were there no other young men to whom she could have entrusted the frightening fact that she believed she had killed her husband? He *was* her husband, I suppose? Not that it matters, if your version is correct. Are you sure she knew nothing about you?'

'I suppose she had seen me, and thought I – thought I looked all right, if you know what I mean –'

'I know exactly what you mean, child. But did the course of events bear out this naïve assumption?'

Harben, to his disgust, discovered himself to be flushing.

'In other words, am I a beast or a fool?' he responded. 'I suppose, to a psychologist, one's bound to be one or the other!'

She grinned.

'To continue,' she went on. 'You connived at what, next day, you believed must, after all, have been a crime; you have omitted to communicate with the police, although you have suffered a murderous attack which you connect, in some way, with the girl – '

'Not with the girl; with the house. With the men who, *I know*, have been in and out of it all summer!'

'Have it your own way, child. You now come to me to get you out of a mess.'

'That's hardly fair – ' began Harben.

'True. It is not fair at all. But you did intend to consult me, didn't you?'

'Yes. I wanted your advice.'

'Do you still want it?'

'Yes, of course, please.'

'Join the Navy or the Port of London Air-Raid Precautions Service, and forget the whole thing.'

'I've written to the Admiralty already, putting myself and my boat at their disposal. There is talk of using little ships for coast work. I'd be useful at something of the sort. There's hardly an inch of the coast I don't know, and know pretty well.'

'There you are, then! You don't want any advice! You've solved the problem for yourself.'

'But it seems like running away. I object to people dabbing at me with oars and boathooks when I've done them no harm and wouldn't know them from Adam if I saw them. Besides, there's the whole mystery of the thing. I confess to my fair share of curiosity, and this is the oddest affair I've ever been mixed up in, and if I don't find out what it's all about I'll go haywire, sooner or later. It's the sort of thing that nags at one, you know.'

His hostess regarded him with sympathy. Then she seemed to make up her mind.

'I'd like to have a look at that house,' she said. 'What do you say to tomorrow?'

'You don't want *me* to come, do you?'

'Nothing would please me better, but never mind. If I manage to contact your mermaid, that will be better still. Sister Mary Sebastian is well enough now to be left to the servants for a day, the boys and Sister Mary Dominic are going blackberrying, and you can go with them and see that the boys don't trespass, so I think I can take a day off with a perfectly clear conscience.'

'A lot you care about a clear conscience!' said Harben, looking very much alarmed. His hostess grinned, and took him into her house. She knew quite well that nothing would keep him away from the house by the river on the morrow.

'One moment ma'am,' said Pirberry, 'if I may interrupt. This is all before I came into the business, isn't it?'

'It is,' agreed Mrs Bradley. She might have added, had she known the expression, 'so what?' She did not know it, however, and favoured her questioner with an interrogative grin.

'What I don't understand,' said Pirberry, 'is why, at this point, you suspected Mr Harben of murdering the old gentleman in the dressing-gown.'

'Have I indicated, then, that I suspected him?'

'Well, ma'am, you seem to have provided him with every excuse not to return to that house when you went to see it, and yet you state that nothing would have kept him away.'

'That doesn't show that I suspected him of murder. I did, however, suspect him of a certain amount of deceit.'

'You mean that the young lady, when she came to the tub as he described, was not a stranger?'

'I don't see how she could have been. But I did not question him on the point. It was not my business. I had acted only as mother-confessor. I did think, however, that he might have his own reasons for wanting to revisit that house and in company with a reliable witness.'

'Meaning yourself, of course, ma'am. You mean he'd hidden the body himself, and wanted the house looked into so that, if need be, you could afterwards be called upon to swear that the body wasn't there. Equally, you now believe we've found it in the Rest Centre. The bit about the dressing-gown shows that.'

'It doesn't prove it, of course, but it's a pointer.'

'And a pretty good one, ma'am, as I agree now I've heard this story. All this you've told me would certainly add up with a jury, I haven't the slightest doubt.'

'Nor I,' said Mrs Bradley. 'But what convinces a jury is not necessarily evidence, you know. And the question is, can a jury really add?'

## CHAPTER TEN

## *Seekers*

The first thing which struck Harben about the house by the river was its neglected and dingy appearance. It seemed impossible that it could have changed so much until he remembered that he was comparing it with the spick and span exterior and cheerful modern comfort of *The Island*.

The windows were dirty and rain-streaked, the wistaria clusters were gone. The paint had blistered in the sun and was peeling off the pillars of the doorway. Harben entered the house by pushing back the catch of a downstair window with the blade of a strong, short knife. Then he climbed in, and opened the door to Mrs Bradley.

He thought at first that the house, inside, was just as he had left it, but, as they began to explore, he was soon aware that he had been right in imagining that it had had other tenants since the departure of himself and Leda. There were cigarette ends, of two different makes, in the drawing-room hearth, and the bed on which the old man's body had lain, and from which it had so mysteriously disappeared, had been stripped of its coverlet and blankets.

Apart from this, nothing had been removed and nothing damaged, so far as he could tell, but he had no inventory of the contents of the house, and no clue to any furnishings or appurtenances beyond those of the rooms he had seen on his previous visits.

He was interested to watch the reactions of his companion. She neither poked nor pried, and yet he felt certain that no detail, however trivial, escaped her notice or would remain unregistered by her memory. She said nothing for some time, but followed him from room to room, upstairs and down, from

the hall to the attics, and back again, doing nothing but sniff the
close air.

When they reached the hall floor again she said:

'Cellars.'

Harben objected that there would be no cellars in a house so
close to the river, but he led the way down a steep and dark
little staircase to the kitchen, which he had not previously seen.
It was a low-ceilinged, semi-basement room, and a scullery of
about the same size, and having the appearance of a large,
square, stone-flagged dungeon, adjoining it on the west.

A door opened out of the scullery on to the bottom of a
rockery, and there was a flight of ugly little brick-built steps
leading up to the level of the garden. Harben unbolted the
scullery door and mounted the steps to a path. The garden was
unkempt and overgrown, and there was a yellow, wet patch in
the long, untidy grass where something heavy and rectangular
had lain. Harben went back to his companion, and found her on
hands and knees on the scullery floor, examining it with the aid
of a powerful torch.

'Worms,' she said; and Harben shuddered at the word, and
saw – or thought he saw – what had been removed from the
garden.

'It's the size of a coffin,' he said. The little old woman got up
and brushed down her skirt.

'In the garden?' she asked. Harben was surprised at the
question. He did not realize until a good deal later that he was
himself being subjected to the same close analysis and searching,
relentless scrutiny as the house he had brought her to see. 'I still
think there's a cellar,' she went on. 'It ought to be easy to locate
it, unless they've blocked up the entrance and made another for
themselves.'

She left him, and went into the kitchen. He wondered what
train of thought was in her mind, and followed her to try to find
out. She was bending over the kitchen hearth, her torch in play
on the hearthstone, but, when he came in, she switched off and
went to a cupboard.

The door swung back, revealing shelves of food, much of it
gone bad. The meat was crawling with maggots. Harben stepped

71

back, but his companion appeared to be oblivious of any unpleasantness, and began to remove the bottles which littered the floor.

Overcoming with some difficulty a feeling of sick repulsion for the crawling life around him and over his head, Harben stooped down to help her, but she said at once, interrupting the chivalrous attempt:

'Touch nothing. I'm wearing gloves. Put your handkerchief over your hand if you want to help.'

He obeyed her, anxious to bring the nauseating task to an end.

When all the bottles were out she switched on the torch and examined the filthy floor inside the cupboard. It was six feet square, and in the middle was a trapdoor. She lifted it up. It came back on unrusted hinges, and disclosed a wooden ladder. This led steeply down into the blackness which shone with slime.

'Here we are,' she said, in satisfied tones. 'You stay up here, and keep watch, whilst I go down. I wonder what depth of water there is at high tide?'

She descended, but not very far. Harben was anxiously combing his hair for maggots. He said nothing, and his companion stood on the ladder, her head just below the level of the pantry floor, and flashed her torch downwards at the water. Then she descended a couple of feet or so, but soon came up again.

'We must wait for low tide. There's nothing more to do until then,' she said. 'You go out and get a meal, and meet me here again at half-past four.'

'A meal!' said Harben, leading the way to the kitchen door. 'My stomach's completely turned by those horrible maggots!' He thought he would never forget the crawling mess.

'Ah, yes, the maggots,' she said. She cackled suddenly. 'There is no speech nor language where their voice is not heard.' To Harben's horror, she returned to the loathly cupboard, collected several specimens of the maggots and placed them in an empty matchbox which she took from the pocket of her skirt. Then, carrying the matchbox tenderly, as though it were filled with rubies, she followed him up the staircase to the hall. They went into the room whose windows looked over the river.

Mrs Bradley sat down at the table, took out a notebook, decanted the maggots carefully on to a page, studied them through a small lens, and made a short note.

'I wish you wouldn't gloat on those filthy bugs!' said Harben suddenly.

'*The Yellow Slugs,*' said Mrs Bradley with relish. 'You must have read it.' She put away the lens, restored the maggots to the matchbox and then went out of the room. She was absent for just four minutes, for Harben studied his watch.

'Where did you go?' he asked, when she returned.

'Back to the kitchen cupboard,' she replied. 'We must find some gardening implements and bury that meat.'

'I'll go outside and look for a toolshed,' said Harben. 'There's bound to be something of the sort.'

He went out into the garden and found, at the end of the rockery, a shed made of planks which were falling apart, and having a roof of corrugated iron which had almost rusted away. It was easy enough to see the interior of the shed between the gaps in the planking, and, except for a sack, there appeared to be nothing inside.

There must be a coalshed, Harben decided, for there could scarcely be coal in a cellar which filled at high tide. He looked for another shed, but there was nothing more outside the house. He returned to the scullery, to find that Mrs Bradley had already discovered a spade.

'Here,' she said, handing it to him. 'A good deep hole about half-way down the garden. Whilst you are digging I will arrange to bring out the remains.'

'Where was the spade?' he enquired. She waved a yellow hand towards the kitchen.

'There is a small place through there where brooms and brushes are kept. The spade was with them. It has had earth on it fairly recently, as you can see. You might look round the garden for signs of recent digging. Not that I think you will find any. They would not have been foolish enough to bury the old man here.'

Harben went out with the spade and looked first for a suitable spot for the interment. He had decided upon a good place when a face appeared over the wall and said conversationally;

'Wondered when any of you people were going to do a bit of clearing up. Don't want to complain, of course, but the seeds of your weeds are blowing about pretty thickly, and lots of them must come over the wall, I should think. Come over and help you, if you like. Anything to get the job done. Got to grow food next year, you know. Can't grow food if it's going to be nothing but thistles.'

'Sorry,' said Harben. 'Nothing to do with me. I'm from the sanitary inspector. Complaints about the drains, but it turns out to be some bad meat the last tenants left.'

'Not surprised at anything *they'd* leave,' replied the stranger. 'Foreigners, I should imagine. Not that I've seen them much. Night-birds mostly, I should guess. But haven't I seen you before?'

'I daresay you have,' answered Harben. 'I used to keep a boat at moorings just off here.'

'Ah, that's it, then, I suppose. I've only been here since March, so I shouldn't have known you really. Just thought I'd seen you, that's all. Oh, well! So long! Just thought I'd mention the weeds.'

Harben dug his hole, and then went to tell Mrs Bradley that it was ready. She had transferred the horrid mess they were to bury to a large cardboard box she had found. Harben mentioned the neighbour, and repeated the conversation.

'Interesting,' said Mrs Bradley, transporting her box on the kitchen shovel. 'We had better leave all the windows open for a bit. Foreigners? I wonder what kind of foreigners? Foreigners who move corpses and appear to be night-birds might interest the police, particularly, I should imagine, at a time like this. The girl you met wasn't a foreigner, I suppose?'

'I haven't the slightest idea. I never even heard her surname. She had no foreign accent. I say, don't you think I'd better be the one to carry that box on the shovel? I told that chap I was from the sanitary inspector's place.'

Mrs Bradley handed over the shovel, but walked just behind

him down the path and across the lawn. He had selected almost the centre of a flower-bed under a crumbling wall. It seemed a suitable place, and was eighty feet, at least, from the rockery.

Harben filled in the hole and stamped the earth flat. Then he shovelled loose mould on the top, and, going to the foot of the wall, called over to the man who had spoken about the weeds.

'If you *do* mean you'll give a hand with those weeds, come over. I'm not due back for an hour. If you bring a spade I'll use this one. We could get the thistles cleared out, if nothing else. I hate to see a good garden in such a state.'

Mrs Bradley went into the house. In less than an hour, Harben, perspiring but cheerful, joined her, and said:

'I don't know what to do about this spade. Are you going to bring the police in to dig over the ground for the body? I thought I'd better have that chap in to disturb the ground a bit more, then the foreigners won't notice the place where we buried the rotten meat.'

'Good for you, child. Well, we have had an interesting afternoon.'

'Have you found out anything useful?'

'There are indications that the well or cellar – whichever we choose to call it – is used for some purpose at low tide, but what that purpose is it is vain to speculate until, at low tide, we have seen it.'

'It's pretty nearly low tide now,' observed Harben, looking at his watch.

'That's another thing,' Mrs Bradley remarked. 'That clock upstairs in the hall – the grandfather – is an eight-day clock. It is going. Did you happen to notice?'

'It sounds as though we had better get out of here before it's dark,' suggested Harben.

'I agree, but I want to make that trip down the cellar steps before we go. How much longer until the tide is at its lowest?'

'As far as this house is concerned, it's low tide now. Where do I wait? At the top of the cellar steps?'

'You may come down with me if you would like to,' she replied. 'Four eyes are better than two.'

Followed by Harben, she descended into the depths, and soon they stood at the bottom on stone which was dangerously slippery from moss and a small, persistent kind of river weed. She flashed the torch over the floor of a sizeable cellar, part of which they deduced to be built out under the garden rockery.

'And you think the old man was carried down here?' asked Harben.

'There is nothing to prove it,' Mrs Bradley answered. She shone the torch on the dripping, moss-covered walls, and then on the sweating bricks above the line of high water. 'Why *build* a cellar under this house?' she added suddenly.

'And yet you knew you would find one,' Harben observed.

'The body was taken somewhere or other after you had laid it on the bed. They *might* have risked conveying it along the river bank and to a boat, but I do not think so.'

'You say "they", but you really think Leda did it, don't you?' Harben said. 'But *I* don't see how she could. He was a pretty good weight, and had to be brought down the stairs before he could be tumbled into this hole. A girl couldn't do it alone.'

'No, a girl couldn't do it alone,' Mrs Bradley agreed, 'but, on the evidence of the neighbour you spoke to over the garden wall, two persons, at least, have had access to the house since the old man's death, and one of them must surely be a man, since, had they been women, the neighbour would have mentioned it, I think. Well, there is nothing very much for two of us to do down here. Do you think you had better go up the steps and keep watch? It would be awkward for us both to be trapped down here when the tide comes in again.'

Harben had been thinking of this for himself, and willingly returned to the kitchen. No one disturbed them, however. He policed the house for twenty minutes whilst Mrs Bradley minutely examined the cellar, and, later, the kitchen, from which she took a Bible in Spanish and a volume of Spanish verse.

'Any luck?' Harben asked, when she came up.

'Yes, just a little perhaps. There is an entrance from the river bank to the cellar, under a flight of stone steps leading up from the strand. There are the dragging marks of a chain across the moss. A kind of sluice-gate can be dropped, and is dropped now, across the entrance.'

'But what would be the object of getting to the river bank that way?'

'I don't know, child. I don't even know whether, at the present day, there is any object at all. The house is about two hundred years old, and the cellar may be much older. Political prisoners were kept, in Tudor times, at the nobleman's house on the other side of the bridge, I believe, were they not? A handy dungeon, which would fill at high tide, and from which the drowned bodies could readily be removed as the tide went down, might have come in very handy, so near such a house. Who knows? At any rate, I shall conclude, until we have evidence to contradict it, that the old man's body was removed from the house this way, whether Leda helped move it or not.'

'You still think she helped to move it?'

'I still reserve judgement, child. The chances are that she did not. But until we know *why* the body was moved, we shall get very little further with the mystery. Did you examine the body?'

'Not as a doctor would have done. There wasn't blood about; that's all I can swear to, I'm afraid. – Oh, except that the old fellow had been sick.'

'On his dressing-gown?'

'No, only on the floor.'

'How do you know it was he?'

Harben stared at her for a moment; then he said:

'I suppose I don't really know it; but don't you think it was all to do with his fall? I didn't notice it at first, not even the smell. The window was open. I shut it because it seemed funny to have a window wide open in a room where a man was dead. And I drew the curtains across. That's when I saw the vomit on the floor.'

'Interesting,' said Mrs Bradley. 'Shall we go?'

## CHAPTER ELEVEN

## Encounter

Harben's dreams were confused that night, but one image in them persisted. He was in a boat, alone, on a wide, dark ocean, when a mermaid came swimming on a luminous track from a solitary star, and clutched at the gunwale with greenish, long, thin fingers. Her hair was one with the night, and her face was so wild and strained as to be unrecognizable, but he knew in his heart that it was Leda, and that, although she was a mermaid, she was drowning and he alone could save her. He knew that he could save her, but, in the dream, he dare not.

He woke in a sweat, to find that it was morning.

He got up and dressed, and went out to look at the river. The garden was nebulous and strange, for a thick white autumn mist lay over the bushes and the trees, and smoked up out of the lawn. Above the water the mist was as thick as teased wool.

There seemed to be about six inches of clear, unmisted air, however, between the river surface and the eddying whiteness above. The face of the water was dark, and, stooping and peering, he could see for some distance ahead. For the first few seconds he stood quietly, every fibre stretched, and thought of the murderous attack he had suffered on a previous misty morning. But very soon this nervous tension left him, and he decided to skirt the neighbouring garden and walk as far as the weir.

The wide, shallow steps from the garden went down to the bed of the river. Almost beside them, less than three yards to the left; a cut had been made in the bank and a very small boathouse built. Just as he came to this boathouse the sun came bright, and the mist began to roll off the face of the garden and, hanging about the trees for a minute or two, was swept away on a breeze which blew suddenly strong from the east.

On the steps was seated a girl. She looked so marble-white

and sat so still that she might have been sculptured there; but the moment the mist rolled back, she slid soundlessly into the water, and began to swim lazily downstream.

Believing she had not noticed his approach, Harben pulled off his clothes, dived cleanly into the river, and set himself to swim after her. He knew the deceptive speed of the long, slow stroke she used, and went his hardest. They passed the garden banks and the pleasant lawns, gained the bend, and a gravelled sweep at the foot of a yellowing water-meadow, passed elms and the thickets of bramble, the patches of careless willow-herb and the tangles of bearded thistle. Slackening, Leda swam to the gravel stretch on the outside bend, and waited for Harben to come up.

'You went back to the house,' she said. It was not a question. Her eyes were as clear as water, and had bright brown flecks in them, like the sun on a stream.

'Yes,' he answered. 'Why not? And where the devil did you get to? Why did you run away, anyhow? And what are you doing down here?'

'I came to find you,' she answered, disregarding the other things he had said. 'We shall need to be very careful. They think you're dead, I believe.'

'I ought to be dead,' he answered. He told of the men in the boat. She raised herself on her arms in the shallow water, and lay on the surface as a fish, with flickering fin, will lie on the bottom among weed.

It was extremely cold, but Harben, fascinated, watched her; traced the wide, flat shoulder, the strong white arms, the sweet, full curve of the throat and the long hands splay-fingered on the gravel, rippled over the movement of the river.

With a flick of her hand, she was away. He could not have said how she did it, or when she began to swim. He knew only that the long fingers must have pressed themselves into the stones to gain the first impetus for flight. In the flash of a fish's tail she was in midstream, and in water deep enough for swimming. The long, straight legs did not move until she was out of his reach, but the little body, turning in one beautiful, fluid movement, like a mermaid's, had eluded in a moment. The water streamed in her wake, then closed behind her, as though it would protect what was its own. Harben plunged forward, and was after her desperately fast, although he knew that he would not come up with her again unless she willed it. She went on swimming downstream, and the distance increased between them, but still he pursued her doggedly, a gleam of hope in his mind. A mile downstream was a lock. She would have to land before she got there. Another thought struck him. In the water she was more than his match, but there was never a swimmer yet who could match a runner on the bank.

Regardless of the fact that he was naked, for the river banks were deserted, but realizing that in less than a hundred yards he could overtake her, he swam to the bank, climbed out, and ran along the grassy edge of the river. The wind on his cold, wet body cut like knives.

The girl soon knew that he had played this move, for she turned, before he came up, and made for the opposite bank.

'Got you!' said Harben, exultant. The tangle of blackberry and thistle, and the low-growing, thorny shrubs, had the effect he foresaw. Panting, afraid, and trapped, she waited for him to join her. He dived, with a long, clean movement, half-way across the stream and was soon on the grass beside her. His madness fell away at her obvious fear.

'I'm not going to hurt you,' he said.

She slid into the water again. Harben, unprepared for this manoeuvre, was caught at a disadvantage. He plunged in after her, but he had not gone a dozen yards before she had covered forty. He climbed out again on to the open, grassy bank he had been deluded into leaving before, but by the time he reached the boat-house he had lost her. He swam ashore to the steps, pulled his trousers over his wet and chilly body, and cantered up to the house. He encountered his hostess on the doorstep.

'*Now* what have you been up to?' she demanded.

'I suppose it's of no use to lie to you,' said Harben. 'I've seen Leda. And I want to see her again. I'm going to see whether I can meet her at the house. I suppose I'm a fool to go – '

'But you're going,' said Mrs Bradley. 'Yes, you *are* a fool. But I suppose you've made up your mind.'

'Well, I'm afraid so,' he said.

'"The expense of spirit in a waste of shame,"' observed his hostess austerely. 'Well, for goodness sake, take my revolver. Remember those cigarette ends and the meat, and those men in the boat.'

'And the eight-day clock,' said Harben.

'Of course, it's quite obvious,' said Pirberry, 'that one of 'em knew the other one had done it, and – '

'All in good time,' said Mrs Bradley. 'What the soldier said isn't evidence, remember.'

'Well, you've indicated one thing pretty clearly, ma'am. You yourself weren't afraid of this young fello. *You* didn't think him a murderer.'

'I certainly didn't think he would murder *me*.'

'Evidently not, ma'am, else you'd hardly have gone down that cellar, leaving him up at the top.'

'One thing I gained without his knowledge, Inspector. Something to rejoice your official heart.'

'Finger-prints, ma'am, I presume?'

'I should think I have the prints of everybody who has ever been in that house. I had plenty of opportunity whilst he was in the garden. You shall have them. They might come in useful.'

'Prints are always something,' said Pirberry.

'Even if only a snare and a delusion,' said Mrs Bradley. 'Oh, and the Spanish Bible and the volume of poetry had the name Inez Hueza on the fly-leaf.'

'That helps a lot, ma'am, said Pirberry.

'Don't be ungrateful,' retorted Mrs Bradley.

## CHAPTER TWELVE

## *Tryst*

The night with the war-time black-out not yet two months in existence, seemed almost incredibly dark. Harben knew the riverside path by heart, but he found himself groping and stumbling between the bridge and the first of the riverside houses, and at one point he crashed into a bench which he had forgotten, and badly bruised his right shin.

He went cautiously after that, for fear of walking over the edge of the bank and into the river.

All was quiet until he got to the inn. From within came the sound of voices in cheerful talk. Dunkirk was months ahead. The popular songs were still about rabbits running, and about hanging washing on the Siegfried Line. Harben was tempted to go in. It was almost closing time, but there would be a chance of getting a drink and some friendly conversation. He pushed open the door, dodged round the black-covered light-trap partition just inside it, and found himself blinking in the white dazzle (as it seemed to him after the darkness) of electric light in the bar.

There was another thought which had occurred to him. He was already impatient at Admiralty delays and circumlocutions. He wanted to get into the war. He might get advice, he thought, at the inn, of how best to use his knowledge and a gift for navigation. He had heard talk of motor torpedo-boats, for instance; just the kind of craft that he could handle.

He looked round the well-filled bar and lighted immediately upon Woods, a crony of his, a man whom he had known for years as a yachtsman.

'Hullo, Stephen,' he said. Woods, a teak-faced, bearded man of fifty with a high, little feminine laugh, made room for him on the corner bench which he occupied, and Harben set down the beer he had bought and enquired what the other was doing.

'A.R.P. firefloats, old man. Great fun. Why don't you join us?'

'Well, I'd thought of the Navy. Small stuff, you know. There ought to be something I could do.'

'Well, why not join us first, and then see how things work out? This picnic won't last six months. Everyone betted that London would be in ruins by the end of last October, but you see, not a thing has happened. The Jerries have got cold feet, I should rather fancy.'

'That's fool's talk,' said Harben, taking a drink of beer. 'Look here, I'll see you tomorrow, if your push will let me join. It's better than nothing, and does at least start me off in my own element, as it were. Oh, and by the way – I'm on rather a peculiar assignment tonight. You might ring up this number in the morning, round about ten, and ask them whether I got back all right. Would you mind?'

He gave Woods Mrs Bradley's Kensington number, knowing that her servants there would ring through to *The Island* as soon as they got the message. Woods copied down the number into his A.R.P. notebook, looked interested and inquisitive, but did not obtain any satisfaction for his natural curiosity. He was not the man to ask questions, and, as it was closing time, they finished their drinks, and Harben accompanied his friend as far as the bridge, and then retraced his steps towards the house.

The night seemed as dark as pitch, and although his eyes grew accustomed to the blackness a little, he was mortally afraid of missing the house in the dark.

Just as he came abreast of the almshouses his heart contracted suddenly and began a curious thumping. He had half a mind to turn back. An older man, a wiser man, or a man more laggard in love might well have given in to such a thought. He could see the house from where he stood. Someone with a torch was standing on top of the steps in front of the door. The torch was a powerful one. It illuminated the pillars of the entrance and threw a tremendous shadow on the porch. It was not possible to see whether the shadow was that of a man or a woman.

He stood, drawn back in the gateway which led to the almshouses, and waited for two or three minutes.

The torch-bearer came down the steps and walked away

rapidly, with resounding masculine footsteps, in the direction of the slipway at the opposite end of the path.

Harben gave him five minutes. Then he went forward, mounted the steps, and knocked.

A scuffling sound came from within, and Leda's voice said loudly and in fear:

'Who's there? Is that the Warden?'

'Yes,' said Harben, disguising his voice. 'I want to see you a minute.'

'Is it the black-out?'

'No.'

'Gas-masks?'

'No. Open up, please. I can't waste time.' He was certain someone was with her and that her questions were put to deceive this other person, whoever it was.

'I can't let you in at this time of night. I'm alone in the house,' she said. Harben opened the letter-box and peered through it into the hall. No black-out curtain was up, but the hall was not lighted.

He took a chance, and whispered through the open letter-slit:

'It's David. Let me in Leda. Don't be afraid.'

'I can't,' she whispered. 'Go away.'

'Are you in any danger?'

'No, I don't think so. But *you* may be if you come in.'

'I don't care. Open the door.'

'No, no! If you love me, go! Come back in about an hour. They'll be gone by then!'

Having no option, he went. He groped his way down the steps by counting them and keeping a hand on the wall. Then he turned west towards the bridge. He scarcely knew what to do with himself for an hour. He was tempted to watch the house from a cautious distance, but time passed slowly, and if, when Leda's visitors left the house, a torch were flashed on him and he were recognized by one of the men (for instance) who had attacked him from the boat at Helsey Marsh, it would complicate an already complicated and dangerous business to the point where it might be impossible to unravel the tangle.

He waited for approximately five minutes, therefore, at the

foot of the steps, whilst these other reflections passed through his mind. Then he went back towards the bridge. The riverside pub was closed. People were drifting over the bridge homewards. Beyond the bridge loomed the black bulk of the gasworks, darker than the very dark sky. Under the bridge, on whose parapet he leaned for twenty minutes before crossing the river to the quiet road beyond, the stream flowed on like black oil.

He guessed the time, having no watch. People jostled against him in the darkness, for he had no torch. At last he recrossed the bridge, took the sloping little road to the riverside, and after losing his way in a turning he had forgotten, found the narrow riverside path and made his way very slowly back to the house.

He knocked, and Leda let him in and took his hand to guide him along the hall. She pushed open the dining-room door. Harben went in. The room was empty.

The grate was empty, too. So much he had time to notice before Leda came in and shut the door. The cigarette ends were gone, and, with them, he took leave to assume, the only evidence that two people, other than himself and his very strange hostess, Mrs Bradley, had been to the house after Leda and he had left it.

The girl came over to the fireplace and sat down. She smiled at him, her green eyes deepening in the way that he remembered, her long mouth stretched and narrow, and her long hands laid along the polished arms of the chair.

'Melisande; Sirena; Pamphiles; Vivien,' said Harben, under his breath; and suddenly, for no reason, he was afraid of this amphibious, green-haired girl who had forced herself into his life.

'*The blanket of the dark,*' he said aloud. He thought of witches, and of their familiar spirits, and found himself shivering at the thought. She noticed it; the smile faded. She leaned forward, looked concerned, the witchcraft gone from her eyes and her long, thin mouth.

'Darling, you're cold. Come on! Let's have a fire.' She went out and brought a portable gas-fire back. She fixed it on to the tap and then went out for a little vessel of water to put before it. 'Water,' she said, as one invoking a god, and, to Harben's discomfort, she smiled at him – the witch's smile again. The hair began to prick on his neck. He was suspicious of the house, of the hour – it was close on midnight – and, keenly, now, of her. He said:

'Now, what are you up to? Why did you get me to come here? And who else is in the house with us?'

She did not answer immediately, and when she did, her remark was not what he expected.

'David, marry me, will you?'

'What are you up to?' asked Harben. 'What's the game? Who's been to live here since you and I went away? There was food in the cupboard gone bad. It hadn't been there very long – certainly not since you and I left, just after Whitsun.'

She looked at him, her green eyes flickering.

'I don't know what you're talking about,' she said, 'and I don't know because . . .'

But the reason was lost to Harben. He heard the creak of the door and glanced across. The girl got up. The door began to open very slowly. Harben, groping wildly for Mrs Bradley's revolver, discovered he had left it behind. He never saw who came in, or how many there were. Just as he stepped out to pick up a chair to make a fight for it, the room shot gold and black at him. He clutched at the chair, but crashed. He remembered watching the floor come up towards him. Then there was nothing at all.

'You mean that's *his* story,' said Pirberry.

'Wait,' said Mrs Bradley. 'There is more. Believe it or not, as you please.'

'The whole yarn, so far, proves that they were in love, Mr Harben and this rather peculiar young lady,' said Pirberry slowly. 'The old bloke, obviously the husband, is done in by one or other of 'em – possibly by both, on the lines of the Thompson-Bywaters case . . .'

'A dangerous example to cite,' said Mrs Bradley.

'Anyway, it hangs together very nicely, ma'am. I should put it that Mr Harben killed the old man, he and the girl between them got rid of the body, and some relations of the dead man got wise to what had happened, but couldn't prove it.'

'How do you make your last deduction?' asked Mrs Bradley.

'Because they laid for him, ma'am. If they'd had proof, they'd surely have come to *us*.'

Mrs Bradley cackled.

# BOOK FOUR

## Ulysses

*

Call not thy wanderer home as yet
Though it be late.
Now is his first assailing of
The invisible gate.
Be still through that light knocking. The hour
Is thronged with fate.

George William Russell ('A.E.')

---

### CHAPTER THIRTEEN

## *Castaway*

Harben had a long, circumstantial dream. He received the impression that he must have been drunk the night before. His head ached, he felt sick, his mouth seemed filled with grit, and he had neither bodily strength nor will-power.

The bed on which he was lying gave a series of slight bounces, then seemed still to be moving, but smoothly this time. After some seconds, but before he had opened his eyes, it settled and became steady.

He sat up and looked about him. The pain just above his eyebrows was agonizing. He could not recognize his surroundings. He knew he was not on the tub; neither was he in a house. He closed his eyes again, overcome by a feeling of nausea. It was too great an effort to think, or to try to remember how he had come where he was.

Two men entered the narrow space in which his bunk was placed. He opened his eyes, realized that both were strangers to him, and closed his eyes again. Beyond a vague impression that one of them was in uniform, he had gained nothing from his brief inspection.

A voice said:

'I told you not to hit him too hard. All these intellectuals have skulls like egg-shells. A fine thing if, after all our trouble, he dies on us.'

'He'll do all right,' said a second voice. 'It's the girl I'm worried about. What can we do with her now?'

'Leave her off here. We must get more juice,' said the first. 'We'll be here at least a couple of hours. I know what these half-breed dagoes are, the lazy tikes! Every day's Sunday with them.'

'How's the time?'

'Just going ten. If we're off by the midday, that will have to do. He can't expect miracles, can he? At least, not until we're involved.'

'He expects all of a man, blood, bones, skin and guts. You don't know who you're working for, my lad.'

'What happens if this chap refuses to play ball?'

'Why, nothing. We can't use pressure. Leave that sort of thing to the Huns. But he'll see it's no use kicking, if he's a sensible fellow. After all, if he hasn't got any money and doesn't know where he is, what can he do? – Play pretty, like everybody else. After all, it's a very good cause.'

'He many not think so.'

'That's his funeral, then. Let's see if we can get him to eat a bit of breakfast. He's been out the best part of twelve hours.'

Harben opened his eyes, sat up with difficulty; and put a hand to his head.

'I'm not asleep,' he said. 'I heard what you said. Where am I?'

'Try guessing,' said the man in uniform, good-humouredly. 'But don't ask questions. It will only give you a worse headache than the one I think you've got already.'

Harben, wincing with pain, put back the blankets and lowered his feet over the side. He tried to stand, but swayed and felt very sick indeed.

'Here, open up! He's going to cat!' said the man in mufti. 'Can't have a mess in here.'

It was then, as the door was opened, and he was half-shoved, half-carried out, that Harben realized that he had been travelling in an aeroplane. His legs gave way. He sank down dizzily on to the ground. The outside air was grateful, however, his captors gave him some water, and almost immediately he began to feel better.

The flat ground on which the aeroplane had landed was a small space artificially levelled, and all around were mountains. He had not the least idea where he was, and long before the 'half-breed dagoes' referred to by his kidnappers had appeared, he was assisted into the plane and told, not at all unkindly, to 'finish sleeping it off'.

'Can you tell me,' he said, in a weak voice which he did not attempt to render stronger, 'what happened to the girl I was with?'

'Yes. She's on board,' replied the man in uniform. He held a short, half-audible colloquy with his companion, then turned to Harben and added, 'You can see her, if you like. But don't make plans to escape, because you'll only land her in the soup. We're perfectly friendly, you know.'

'The war,' began Harben. The man laughed; not unkindly.

'We've got nothing to do with the war,' he said. 'Not the one you're concerned with, anyhow. You'd have laughed to see yourself being carried out of that house in an empty cistern, with the girl on top of you like a couple of rolled-up anchovies.'

'But what's the game?' asked Harben.

'You'll know by tomorrow,' said the man. 'Here's a sight for sore eyes! Look! Now you'll soon feel all right.'

The other man brought in, not Leda, but Sister Mary Dominic. She was as lovely as ever, but was, he noticed, extremely pale, and looked as though she had not slept.

'You?' cried Harben. '*You* got me into this?'

The two men looked at each other, raised their eyebrows, chuckled, and went out of the cabin, leaving the lovers together (for Harben realized clearly in his dream that he was in love with Sister Mary Dominic).

She, lifting her eyes, made answer:

'You don't believe I got you into this trouble? David, I know nothing about it; only what you know – that these men came into the house, and I thought they'd killed you. This is nothing to do with my affairs. I swear to you I know nothing whatever about it!'

He did not know whether to believe her. There was silence. Then some people came up to the aeroplane, and could be heard explaining, in poor English, that they would have to send for the petrol. The two men cursed them, arguing that they could not wait, and that the petrol should have been on the spot, or, at any rate, ready in the village. They were promised speedy service, but one of the men said to the other:

'Better float down with them, and swim them rapidly along. We don't want to spend the night in this filthy hole!' What about *them?*' enquired the other. There was a slight pause, during which the first must have made some gesture – produced a revolver, probably, Harben thought – for the speaker went on. 'Oh, yes. Well, all right, then. I'll go. So long. Only hope they've got the quantity we want! We can't do it on less than five million.'

Harben looked at Sister Mary Dominic, and said angrily:

'Well, whatever you say, you got us into this confounded mess, and you'd better hurry up and get us out. But nothing will persuade me that it wasn't a put-up job!'

She answered, in sulky tones:

'Oh, suit yourself, but shut up!'

At these words she picked up a jug of water and threw it over him, and he awoke. He found himself in an open boat. A wave, slapping over the stern in a following wind, had drenched him, and he was lying in the pool of water it had left. It was broad daylight, and he was out of sight of land. He was alone.

He blinked away his dream and sat up. The boat had no oars, no sail, and no engine. He did not know how long he had been at sea. He found that he was dressed in someone else's clothes, and that all the pockets were empty. There was a small cask in the nose of the boat. He supposed there was water in it. There seemed to be no food.

Beyond a slight feeling of sickness and a bad headache, he felt fit enough, he decided, But he was extremely cold.

The sea was heaving in great grey masses which threatened to engulf his little boat. He raised himself and took hold of the tiller to keep the boat's head to the seas. He realized that he was extremely hungry, and tried very hard to remember when last he had had any food. He strove and strove with himself, but his mind was a blank. He could remember the tub, and the faces of Leda, Mrs Lestrange Bradley, and the nuns flitted across his visual memory like lantern slides at a lecture; but who any of them were, and what they had ever meant to him he had not the slightest idea. Even their names meant nothing, although, as the boat tossed and heaved, and the mountainous seas came rolling terrifically towards him, he repeated them perhaps a hundred times.

He touched the lump on his head, but that meant nothing, either. He supposed he must have got into a fight or met with an accident. He realized that (for the time, at any rate) he had lost his memory, and it seemed to him very odd that he should remember that he ought to have memories, and yet should have mislaid them in this way. But he took comfort, too.

'I *shall* remember,' he thought. 'I'm not so badly off as I might be over it all. I *shall* remember. It's only a question of time.' Besides, he remembered his dream. He could repeat the conversations word for word.

But very soon it also began to be a question of food. The problem of water could be solved, for a short while, by the cask in the nose of the boat. It contained, as nearly as he could judge, about a gallon.

Then there was the question of sleep. He had no idea how long he had been unconscious. People with concussion were sometimes unconscious for two or three days, he believed. True, the boat had not foundered. There was also the argument that it must have been launched from somewhere, but whether from the shore or from a ship he could not tell.

Being philosophical by temperament and by self-training, he decided to sleep when he had to, and trust to luck that the boat would not be swamped.

'After all, I can't do *everything*,' he said aloud. About an hour later, the wind dropped. He was afraid that by morning there would be a flat calm, a dreadful thought to one who had no possible means of propulsion.

The sun set at last, dark came, and, with the knowledge that no vessel he might encounter would carry lights unless she happened to be a non-belligerent, he lay down at the bottom of the boat resigned to the fact that, at any moment of the darkness, he might be run down by a passing monster. It would be idle, he felt, to attempt to convince himself that he was not afraid.

Fatigue and boredom overcame fear, and he slept. When he awoke it still was dark, and he saw a light in the distance. He did not believe it could come from land because of the stringent regulations in force against all lights, especially those on the coast. It must, he argued, be a ship, and a neutral ship. He watched it anxiously. The light drew nearer. Then he could see red from the port-side lamp. The ship was coming towards him. Frantically he searched the pockets of the clothes he was wearing, but there was not so much as a match with which he could attempt to make a signal.

He tried shouting, but the ship held on her course. He tried to estimate her speed, and wondered whether, by taking a chance, and making a long slant towards her, he could possibly swim to her side. But the plan was as wild at its conception, and he did not make the attempt. By morning the seascape was empty, except for himself and his boat. Then, at about the midday, he saw another ship, a squat little tramp with a couple of yellowish funnels and the Spanish flag painted large along her side.

He stood up, rocking the boat, and waved his arms. The tramp altered course. He could see gesticulating figures. Then she shut of her engines but did not lower a boat. He supposed she had not one.

'Badly found. I'll have to swim for it,' he thought. He prepared to abandon his boat, but, as he drifted nearer, and the tramp, making use of the way she still had on her after her engines had ceased, came sucking and slapping towards him, he saw that the crew had grappling hooks on the ends of ropes, and meant to secure the boat.

'Good! I can drive a bargain,' Harben thought. He stood up again, and cried:

'*Amigo! Amigo!*'

Out came the grappling irons, missing his head by inches. He fixed them into the thwarts. The boat was drawn in. Judging his distance, he reached for the rope ladder the tramp was dangling overside. Up he climbed, hand over hand.

It took an hour, and a thousand Spanish oaths, to get his boat on to the deck, but the Spaniards were determined to have it. Harben, fed, washed, and his own clothes left to dry in the galley, was soon dressed in a pair of trousers and an oil-stained blouse belonging to a hybrid but friendly and good-natured gentleman known to his intimates as *El Piojo*, which is, by interpretation, 'The Louse'.

Harben had invented, and was able to tell the captain of the vessel, a well-substantiated story of having been on his way back to England from a Mediterranean cruise on his thirty-ton yacht when war was declared. He related his adventures. The captain, a square-jawed, black-avised man who chewed tobacco continuously, but had, in all other respects, the manners of a somewhat sardonic prince, listened without interruption except that at particularly impressive or incredible points in the narrative he spat overside in an admiring rather than a contemptuous or unbelieving manner, and ejaculated:

'*Hijo de Dios! San Salvador!*' in polite, diplomatic and conciliatory tones. A man to beware of, thought Harben.

'Lastly, there is, of course, my beautiful boat, which I offer you in lieu of passage money,' concluded Harben, in his sufficient but laboured Castilian. The Spaniard continued to smile.

'That is better than nothing,' he agreed; but followed up this polite shrug, to Harben's discomfiture, with the sardonic proverb, 'It is the weak dog which always has fleas.'

Harben was given a berth in the forecastle and went to sleep that night with the knowledge, gained from El Piojo, who seemed to have taken a fancy to him, that the ship was bound for Santander.

'We shall get there in a month or so,' said El Piojo, on deck

95

next morning. 'He goes to Gran Canaria, this ship, to Tenerife, to all those places.' He waved a long, thin, dirty hand with grandeur towards the horizon.

'And after Santander?' said Harben to the captain, later. The Spaniard smiled.

'*Quien sabe? A Dios rogando y con el mazo dando*,'* he replied with magnificent philosophy.

They made Las Palmas, chief port on the island of Grand Canary, in three days, but remained at the mole for less than twenty-four hours. Harben, who had no intention whatsoever of remaining on board for months whilst the little ship tramped for cargo, went ashore to see what Las Palmas had to offer, but came aboard again, as the ship was leaving so soon, after having bathed from the sands of Confital Bay, a pleasant stretch to the north of the city and on the west side of the Ismo de Guanarteme. He had hoped that there might be a chance of obtaining a passage on some ship bound direct for Spain, but the time-limit was too short for him to find out much about the sailings, and he did not intend to risk being left behind at Las Palmas without money or prospects. True, there was the British Consulate, but he concluded that it would be equally ineffective to apply there after he had played a lone hand. As the ship was bound next day for Tenerife, he could, at least, wait until then.

They put off with the tide next morning, having unloaded an innocuous cargo of manufactured goods, and having taken on board a few cases of what the mate, a grim fellow, called Don Juan by the men, and Pico by the captain (to whom, it appeared, he was slightly related by marrige), termed fish manure. They looked to Harben remarkably like gun cases, and he dropped his end of one when they were loading, to see what happened. Don Juan swore at him, and his fellow-labourer, Gomez, a merry little fellow from Barcelona, giggled and said:

'You have greased your palm, no? Or does your honour see mermaids over the side?'

'Mermaids!' said Harben; and everything came back. The case had not burst open, and he was none the wiser from the

* Who knows? Pray to God, and keep on hammering.

sound it made striking the deck. There were fewer than a score of these cases. Even if they had contained rifles, they would not have constituted a dangerous armament, and the mate was either a man without nerves (which was credible enough) or one without a guilty conscience, and that was quite likely too. And there was, of course, the fact that the cases might contain exactly what they were said to contain, although, if this were so, they must have been deodorized by some secret process, thought Harben, sniffing a suspiciously untainted air.

The ship, which could make ten knots without danger to her internal organization, came into the port of Santa Cruz at just about three o'clock. The Mole was long, and something of the shape of a dog's hind-leg, and behind it a range of mountains, which formed the backbone of the island and gave to it its shape, could be seen like steep black battlements against the splendid sky.

It seemed that the ship was expected to stay three days. Some cargo was unloaded on the first of these, the second was declared a holiday, and on the third the intake cargo was to come aboard, brought by mule, said El Piojo, from the south. Harben paid little attention. He was fully occupied with his thoughts.

The road northwards out of the town was along the coast. With his head full of boats and ways of escape by them to England, Harben followed this road on the second day, and came, in about an hour and a half, to the dirty little village of San Andres. Here the road, ceased, and nothing but a rough path led onwards. It skirted a tiny headland and then a slightly larger one, dropped to the coast once more, and terminated, so far as a coastal course was concerned, at another little village called Igueste. At Igueste it turned sharply north to the pine forests on the mountains before leading to the lighthouse on the northern tip of the island.

He had taken another hour to get from San Andres to Igueste. He had left the city at ten. He was hot and extremely hungry, but, beyond the sum of five pesetas, borrowed (without difficulty) from El Piojo – he had not liked to ask more from the good-natured half-breed – he had not a coin in his possession.

There was no inn at Igueste, so he approached a man leading a mule, and asked him for something to eat.

The man stopped, jerked his head round and remarked that he must wait for his ladies. These proved to be two desiccated Englishwomen to whom Harben forthrightly (and, he hoped, ingenuously) addressed himself.

The sight of a young, personable man of their own nationality impressed the Englishwomen favourably, in spite of the fact that he was ragged, although shaven and reasonably clean. They listened to what he had to say, and appeared to accept his story, which was the one he had told already to the captain.

'You had better come down into Tenerife and speak to the Consul,' said the older lady. 'We can't ask him to the hotel,' she added, in what was evidently intended to be a tactful murmur. 'What is it you really want?' she demanded, turning to him again.

'A passage to England,' he replied. 'I intend to join the Navy. I am an amateur yachtsman. But I'm afraid I'll never get back while the war's on, and the Consul can't help me, you see, and I don't suppose you can, either. All I'm asking of you now is a meal. I think, if you gave permission, your man there – '

'Oh, Luis!' said the elder lady. 'I believe he's really a villain. I shouldn't trust him an inch. We never allow him to have anything to do with our food. Dirt, you know! Perfectly poisonous!'

'I could eat what he eats,' argued Harben. He approached the muleteer and said pleasantly:

'*Las señoritas están buenas. No tengo las viandas*a.'

The man grinned amiably, showing broken teeth.

'We men, sir, will eat,' said he, evidently accepting Harben's first remark regarding the goodness of the ladies as permission to sit down and rest. He hitched his mule to a spined and fleshy-leaved plant, sat down, and took from his pocket a very large knife. The younger lady gave a slight scream at the sight of it. The muleteer rose leisurely, went to his mule, and took from one of the panniers a lump of the bread of the island, a kind of dough made from toasted grain and salt, and known as *gofio*. This, and a piece of salt fish resembling cod, proved to be his meal.

He smiled sideways towards his employers. 'They are mad,' he observed kindly. 'They want to go to England to have a part in the war. Express to yourself the extreme idiocy of such a cranky idea!'

Harben laughed, went over to the ladies to assist them from their mules, which, with a temperament inherited from patient forefathers or acquired from contact with their owner, had pulled up behind their tethered companion and were attempting to browse, and observed, with winning courtesy:

'Pray do not be alarmed by our Spanish friend. I am sure he means well, and is an honest and hardworking man.'

'He has nine children, if that means anything,' said the elder lady severely. She had allowed herself to be assisted from her animal, and the Spaniard, putting down his food, came forward, with native politeness, to help the younger lady to dismount.

'Well, I suppose this is as good a place for lunch as any other,' the elder lady observed. She, too, rummaged in the panniers, and produced some packets of food and a bottle of wine.

'Here, Luis,' she said. 'Your cup. *Copa.*'

'*Muchas gracias, señora,*' said the muleteer, pulling out his cup from his pocket. Before he drank, Harben bowed to the ladies. The muleteer crossed himself piously, muttered, '*A Dios*' – although whether to the deity or to the wine Harben was not able to discover – and drained his cup at a gulp.

'He likes wine,' said the elder lady to Harben, 'although, really, they're very abstemious. We've done the dangerous part of the journey this morning, so I don't mind him having it now. We decided not to have lunch until after we had reached the sea-level. It is so much safer.'

'Look here,' said Harben, 'he tells me you want to get back to England. Is that true?'

'Get back?' said the elder lady. 'We came for six months, and that six months expired some weeks ago. But there are no liners to England, so here we shall stay, unless Spain should enter the war. It is all rather tiresome.'

'You will certainly find it difficult to get back while the war is on,' agreed Harben. 'How much money have you?'

'Oh – ' The elder lady looked at him closely. 'Oh, plenty of money,' she said. 'Why, in particular, young man?'

'I want you to buy or hire a small fishing boat,' he said. 'If you do, I'll engage to get you back to England, whenever you wish.'

'Crazy!' said the elder lady, sharply. 'How do we know that you can even steer?'

Harben did not reply. He assisted the ladies to mount, and they all went along the road by the way he had come out that morning. The small debt to El Piojo he was soon in a position to discharge, for the muleteer (well-tipped by the ladies, who, apparently, were usually something niggardly) had given him five pesetas under the impression that Harben's presence on the homeward journey had brought him increased prosperity, as, indeed, there was no doubt it had.

'Go with God, señor,' he had said, when they had parted. 'And come out with us another day. They like you. But a word in your ear. They are old. Even the younger one is fifty.'

'They are rich,' said Harben, 'and, you know the saying – *Caballo grande . . . ande o no ande*. A big horse, whether it goes or not.'

The grinning Spaniard slapped him on the shoulder.


CHAPTER FOURTEEN

## *Voyage Home*

Having committed themselves to the expedition and to his care, the English ladies proved to be surprisingly enterprising and adaptable. They made no secret of their preparations and bought the fishing boat recommended by Harben with a rather pathetic (although, as it happened, a well-founded) faith in his judgment.

She was a clumsy old boat, but Harben had decided that her defects were not such as would, of themselves, seriously prejudice the safety of his passengers. She was overhauled, patched up, given a life-boat and a new set of charts, a compass fitted with an azimuth mirror, a sextant and a pair of dividers, and set out upon her fourteen-hundred mile passage on the first of April – a suitable date, thought Harben, for beginning the hazardous project.

One tremendous piece of luck had been his. Two Englishmen, one man of fifty-four, the other his son, aged twenty-two, had expressed the wish to go with him. They were accustomed to sail their own boat from island to island of the Canaries, had been across to the African coast in her, and north-west to Madeira.

Thus he was able to command the services of a valuable crew, and the women, although he intended that they should take their turn, if only in the galley or as deck-hands, would not be called upon for engine-room duties.

They went nowhere near Madeira itself, but ran in past Lanzarote and tiny Allegranza and then steered by dead reckoning directly northward for the first few hundred miles, and then a point or two east to bring them abreast of Finisterre, from which they could check their position.

Watches were not easy to keep with so very small a ship's company, but the women, true to their blood, proved as effective on deck as in the galley, and the general rule laid itself down that they took watch and watch with the men. The only difference was that they always kept watch together, whereas in the case of the men it was possible only to have one man on deck in addition to the man at the helm.

Rations were fairly short and so was water, since it was considered impracticable to put into port, even in Portugal or Spain.

But the adventure never entered the heroic class, although it afforded two eldery ladies conversation and glory right to the end of their days. The ship made Finisterre on April thirteenth, having been buffeted, but not unduly considering her size, and from there it was, except for colder weather and choppy seas, an easy passage. They kept wide of the Bay of Biscay, and then made north-east for Ushant, but left it, they reckoned and hoped, at least eighty miles to starboard. They gave the Channel Islands as wide a berth as they could, and then turned into the Channel itself, and kept a strict watch for aeroplanes.

But these were the days before the blitz; before Dunkirk; before the capitulation of the French or the invasion of Holland, Belgium and Luxembourg; before the threat of an invasion of England. All seemed calm, even normal, and out in France an English Field Security Officer* stationed at Croise Laroche, just north of Lille, was still keeping fit by doing 'the steeplechase course . . . occasionally in the evenings, on foot, taking all the jumps except the water-jump, while the French A.A. gunners . . .' jeered at his incomprehensible antics.

When the ship reached a point about fifty miles from Start Point, as near as could be reckoned, a council was held while the ship lay hove to. There was no reason why the identity of the ship and her crew should not be known to the coastal patrols of ships and aeroplanes, but if re-entry into the country of their birth could be made without official interference, so much the less bother. This was the general view, including that of the women, therefore it was agreed that the ship should creep coastwards under cover of the night and the crew should get ashore as best they could from the little boat they had taken on board at Santa Cruz.

The women, with the genius of their sex for leaving what Harben referred to as 'the stickier part of the arrangements' to the men, proved remarkably docile and obedient. The ship flew the Spanish flag until she was within the territorial waters of the British Isles, and then this was changed for the Union Jack. Although several aeroplanes were sighted, and two warships passed at a distance of less than a mile, no interference was made and no signals had to be answered.

'Good thing we're a fishing boat. Disarms criticism,' said Harben. 'We'll have a try at running in tonight. I think I know the best place, but, of course, I can't guarantee we won't step straight into sentries or coastguards when we land.'

The voyage had been so uneventful as to prove, after the first few days, rather boring. The ship's company were inclined to welcome the prospect of excitement. Plans were made to scuttle the fishing boat in twenty-five fathoms of water just south of

* Captain Sir Basil Bartlett, Bt. *My First War*. (Chatto & Windus, 1940.)

Portland Bill, so that she could not constitute a danger to shipping; then they would take to the small boat, and get ashore as best they could.

'No minefields along the south coast,' said Harben, hopeful that the information he remembered having acquired from a war atlas during the first few months of the war was still correct, 'and our contraband control ends approximately at the Isle of Wight, I believe. We can land on the Dorset or Devonshire coast and no questions asked, if we're lucky.'*

'Army minefields,' said the older of the men.

'We shall have to chance them if we're going to land this way,' said Harben cheerfully.

'Barbed wire,' said the elderly man.

'Same answer. There are almost bound to be gaps. We must pull the boat in as far as we can, and then lie offshore until the dawn breaks.

'Every man for himself, and the devil help the ladies, you mean?'

They turned and surveyed, with chivalrous misgivings, the thin and elderly backs of the patient women.

'They've done all right so far,' said Harben, on the defensive. 'They're agreeable to scuttling the ship. They say they don't want her any more. And they'd never have got back without us.'

'I'm not arguing,' said the older man. 'Have you arranged for the scuttling?'

'Yes. Raymond and I have everything ready down below. She ought to fill in about a couple of hours. Plenty of time for all of us to get well away before she goes.'

'*Pinta*. It's an unlucky name,' said Raymond, the younger man, referring to the fishing boat they had brought so far and so favourably.

'It won't be, for us,' said Harben. They abandoned ship at

* 'There was the case, a few months later (i.e. later even than October, 1940), of a Middlesex man, week-ending at Torquay, who was swept out to sea in a hired dinghy which capsized. He clung to the boat all night and at daybreak drifted close to the shore. He climbed on to the beach – and no one challenged him.' – Michael Joseph, *The Sword in the Scabbard*. (Michael Joseph, 1942.)

the very first gleam of the dawn. The *Pinta* had been filling for about half an hour before they left her. The engine-room was by that time completely flooded. The women, who had been very nervous all night, were helped into the bobbing boat down a rope ladder which they declared, at first, they could not possibly use. They had no portable possessions to speak of, but each lady had put on three sets of clothes, and they had stowed a considerable amount of money – all that they had left – about their persons.

'We may have to climb cliffs,' Harben warned them. The men took turns at the oars. There were two pairs, fortunately, for otherwise the boat would have been exceedingly heavy to row.

The day came slowly to birth. The tide was setting strongly towards the land, and washed the boat in. The soft April day unfolded, disclosing a sandy beach, cliffs, but not high ones, and, on a distant headland, the misty, pinkish haze of the early morning.

They beached the boat and landed. It had been arranged that they should separate as soon as they had disembarked, but the two women showed an instinctive inclination to keep abreast of the men and to follow their tactics.

Harben's first thought was to get away from the beach, which he felt quite certain would be mined. Fortunately this impression was not put to the test. They all reached the cliffs and scaled them – it was an easy climb up – and at the top encountered wire, but so sagged and fallen with the pressure of winter weather that it was not difficult to cross it and gain the short turf of the land at the top of the cliffs.

The father and son were together, and as perhaps was natural, since, beside being unattached, he was, in a sense, their pensioner, the women remained with Harben, following him up the cliff and accepting his assistance to make the last wild stride which brought them, sprawled on hands and knees, to the top.

He accepted his responsibilities cheerfully, and suggested that it would be as well to follow the footpath near which they found themselves, in the hope that it led to a village.

It led, as it happened, not to a village but sharply downhill to a small shallow lake on the shore of which was drawn up a little boat. Harben stepped into the boat, helped the women aboard, and then pushed off with the boat-hook he found across the thwarts.

He ferried across to the opposite shore, and then, bidding the ladies turn their backs, he stripped, rowed the boat to her moorings, and, splashing into the lake, which had a temperature somewhere (it seemed to him) around freezing point, swam vigorously back to join them.

He dried himself on his shirt, put on his other garments, and, hanging the shirt round his neck in the hope that it would soon dry, he led the way to a broad and sandy beach. Behind it were dunes and scrubby, long, yellowish grass, half-a-dozen bathing huts, a lean-to shed whose faded and washed-out notice-boards indicated that refreshments might be obtained there. There was also a notice put up by the military authorities to point out that the beach was dangerous, and that soldiers were forbidden to bathe there.

The travellers passed inland, still following their path. It led almost back to the lake, skirted a patch of tall reeds, and came out by the banks of a river.

The river wound for a couple of miles across fields, and then passed beside a ruined church. A little further on was a bridge, and, carried by the bridge across the stream, a fairly wide metalled road.

'Looks a little more like home,' said Harben cheerfully; and suddenly stopped dead in his tracks, for, coming out of an inn on the farther side of the bridge, and dressed in ordinary civilian clothes and a soft felt hat, was his erstwhile acquaintance the sardonic and handsome Spanish captain.

Some instinct caused Harben to dart back behind the shelter of the bridge and go to ground there. He could not afterwards find any explanation of this behaviour. He had no reason to fear the Spanish captain, yet his instinct was to avoid him.

The ladies, naturally surprised at Harben's extraordinary conduct, remained on the bridge, and leaned over, gazing at the water, and hoping that their protector had not gone mad. When the road was clear again, they approached him cautiously.

'Did that fellow have anyone with him?' Harben enquired.

'Yes, he was followed by a short, dark man. They looked like foreigners,' said the older woman, staring at him curiously.

'I owe them money,' said Harben, believing, with some confidence that this explanation would suffice to explain his conduct. 'It would be awkward to run into them now.'

'Mr Harben,' said the older woman, 'I know this place where we are. I believe it is not far from Bournemouth. There should be a bus. Shall we say good-bye now, and relieve you of further responsibility?'

'Why, as to that – ' said Harben. But she was conducting a search among her too ample clothing, and paid no attention until she had found what she wanted.

'Will you accept a hundred pounds, and our gratitude, Mr Harben?'

'Good God no!' said Harben. He laughed. 'After you paid for the ship and the stores, and fitted me out with new clothes? No, really, I've plenty of money. I've still four pounds which I saved by bargaining for the fittings. I shall pay these fellows directly I get back to Town. Really, now we're in England, I'm not in the slightest need – But – here comes the bus. Look here – in case I don't see you again – '

He took the older lady by the shoulders and gently kissed her thin cheek.

'You've been bricks,' he said. 'Really you have. It's been a privilege and pleasure to serve you.'

'Well!' said the lady. The bus drew up. The two women boarded it. He wondered, watching the bus out of sight, how they would manage for money to pay their fares. Their wealth, he believed, was all in Spanish pesetas and English pound notes. He did not know that the other lady, in finding the hundred pounds to present to him, had, at the same time brought out the quantity of English small change which, with the spinster's habit in such important matters, she had had secreted ever since her first landing on the Canaries.

He tramped a couple of miles, came to a little village, got on a bus to Bournemouth, and there, having breakfasted, took a ticket for Waterloo. He also bought cigarettes, matches and a newspaper. The date was the nineteenth of April. Altogether he had been absent for more than five months.

'Pretty work,' said Pirberry, grinning. 'What fraction or part of the yarn is true, ma'am?'

'I cannot say. I have not checked it,' said Mrs Bradley mildly. 'The dream, to a psychologist, was interesting.'

'Cleverly worked out, you mean, ma'am?'

Mrs Bradley chuckled.

'Mr Harben is a clever man,' she said. 'What do you make of the Spaniards and the English ladies?'

'Phony, ma'am,' said Pirberry, without hesitation. 'But what did you do when you found the young fellow had disappeared? Did you have a look for him at all? Apart from bringing Sir Beresford into it, I mean, and the little bit *we* did later.'

'You shall hear all,' said Mrs Bradley.

# BOOK FIVE

## Sleuth's Alchemy

*

'Why grass is green, or why our blood is red,
Are mysteries which none have reached unto.
In this low form, poor soul, what wilt thou do?
When wilt thou shake off this pedantry,
Of being taught by sense and fantasy?
Thou look'st through spectacles; small things seem great
Below; but up unto the watch-tower get,
And see all things despoiled of fallacies

John Donne

---

### CHAPTER FIFTEEN

## *Familiars*

To say that Mrs Lestrange Bradley was perturbed by the disappearance of her guest would be an over-statement. It was Sister Mary Dominic who perturbed her, for Sister Mary Dominic fretted over his absence, and even that relaxed and cheerful person the humorous and placid Sister Mary Sebastian, O.P., said that she felt no good could come of 'this running about at nights'.

'It is not as though he were a *depraved* young man,' she naïvely added. Mrs Bradley agreed, although she thought it possible that her own definition of the word might not coincide exactly with that of the nun.

She had made a sufficiently accurate estimate of Harben's character, however, to believe him to be capable of ill-considered and impulsive conduct which might readily lead him into danger. This belief was not in any degree lessened by the telephone call which she had received from her Kensington house, for the faithful and unforgetful Woods had done exactly as Harben had asked him to do, and had rung through in the morning. Mrs Bradley's servants had then transmitted the message to *The Island*.

Upon receipt of Woods' message, Mrs Bradley rang up the police, and set out upon an investigation of the most probable scene of Harben's disappearance. From his previous descriptions of the house, she did not anticipate any difficulty in finding it.

The riverside was lively and colourful, the autumn air brisk and cool. The tide was high, and a little creek, which had been a muddy trickle a few hours earlier, now carried boats at moorings, and a depth of five feet of water.

Several people noticed the small, black-haired, incongruously clad old woman who walked up to the door of the double fronted, empty house, but no one appeared to be more than ordinarily interested in her movements.

From a bunch of keys in her possession she selected own which provided dignified admittance by way of the handsome old door. She had discovered this useful key on her previous visit – or, rather, had discovered that it fitted.

In the hall Mrs Bradley stood still and sniffed the air. Then she withdrew into a small recess between the hall-stand and the front door, and, producing a small handbell, removed plasticene from its stopper and clattered it as loudly as she could. It did not ring, as some of the plasticene still adhered, but it made sufficient sound to startle the inhabitants of the house.

These proved to be, once again, the small grey monkey which came chattering out of one of the downstair rooms to swing itself on to the carved post which supported the banisters, and the parrot, which walked in a stately manner out of the dining-room, bowed twice in the direction of the front door, and observed theatrically, 'No, not Cripplegate, old boy,' several times in succession.

Mrs Bradley, from her post of vantage, surveyed the bird and the small mammal, and then swung the bell-clapper again. The monkey gave a short scream and bounded away up the stairs. The parrot walked with a comical strut to the foot of the staircase, appeared to look up to where the monkey cowered and gibbered at the top, then lifted one claw and said genially:

'A dirty night at the *Cat's Whisker*, old boy. Old boy, old boy, old boy.'

Mrs Bradley stepped out from her hiding-place and proceeded to explore the house. The parrot accompanied her, except downstairs to the kitchen. The monkey remained where he was until she began to mount the stairs. Then he fled, screaming with fear and annoyance, to the floor above.

There was no clue to Harben. Mrs Bradley searched and explored, sounded walls, opened cupboards and clothes chests, and spent, altogether, nearly two hours in the house. A minor mystery was the fact that the front door, which she distinctly remembered closing, was wide open when she came down again from the attics.

She examined the fastenings, but there seemed to be nothing amiss. The telephone was in order, so she rang through to Sister Sebastian to say that she would not be back that night, and then, for the second time, rang up her friend, the Assistant Commissioner, to suggest that the local police might like to keep watch on the house. She did not tell him the story over the telephone, but promised to give it him later.

Nothing happened; and Scotland Yard was gently humorous over the telephone in the morning. Harben, however, did not appear, and no news came of him. Mrs Bradley, ignoring official gibes and rude suggestions, suggested, in her turn, that the police might like to undertake to help her to trace her young friend. She also gave them Harben's description of Leda.

The Assistant Commissioner arrived in person at three in the afternoon to find her talking to the monkey (which had adopted her fairly readily once it had been fed) and, alternately, listening to the parrot, whose conversation seemed to her full of interest. The Assistant Commissioner came alone, and was careful to explain that he was paying a private, friendly, strictly unofficial visit. She grinned, and explained that the local police had frightened away all visitors.

'And now, what *is* all this?' the Assistant Commissioner demanded. 'This is no time to amuse yourself, you know.'

Mrs Bradley disclaimed any frivolous purpose in enlisting the support of the police, and told of Harben's message and disappearance, and added that she was anxious about the young man. She described him minutely and well, and told of the visit which he and she had already paid to the house. She described the night she had spent, and added that whatsoever dark secrets the house contained remained hidden. Her only discovery, which she suggested might be pigeon-holed at the back of the official mind for future reference if necessary, was that, since her last visit, persons unknown had made their way into the garden. The rectangle of damp and yellowish grass which she and Harben had seen, was covered partly by a large zinc cistern. That it was not the original container which had occupied the site was clear, for it had an almost square base, whereas the rectangle of yellowish grass was both longer and narrower than the cistern, and showed for nearly ten inches at either end of it.

Upstairs, in a cupboard at the top of the steps to the attics, was the cistern belonging to the house. It was in good order. The Assistant Commissioner, still not at all impressed, helped Mrs Bradley to inspect it.

Out in the garden they moved the empty cistern and measured the yellowish patch on which it stood. The measurements certainly suggested those of a coffin, but, as the Assistant Commissioner unnecessarily and facetiously pointed out, to stand an empty coffin in one's back garden does not, in itself, constitute an offence against the law.

Even Harben's disappearance he was at first inclined to take lightly. He observed that Mrs Bradley had known nothing whatever about the young man before he turned up at *The Island* in charge of the nuns and the boys, and, upon her retorting that the young man was a fairly well-known novelist, he laughed.

She remained unruffled, and showed him the entrance to the cellar, demanding, as she did so, whether he had ever seen a cellar flap made in a pantry floor.

He replied that he did not see why the opening should not be where it was, but she retorted to this that it was evident to people who had eyes in their heads that the pantry floor had originally been of stone.

'Well, let's go down,' he said. It proved impracticable to carry out this suggestion, for the tide was in, and the cellar was half-full of water. 'Now, that *is* odd,' he admitted, closing the trap and dusting the knees of his trousers. 'But what's odd isn't necessarily criminal, you know, and, of course, you've only the word of this young fellow, who probably lives in a world of moonshine, anyhow, that he's ever been attacked and that there was anything strange about this house.'

'Well,' said Mrs Bradley, 'be that as it may, I'd like very much to know where David is.'

'Oh, we'll bear it in mind. If the local people don't make any objection, I'll give you Pirberry for a bit. You like him, and have worked with him before. But I can't see anything to go on. You might let us know if Harben turns up all right. And now – what about dinner tonight?'

But Mrs Bradley refused the invitation. The Assistant Commissioner, she noted with inward amusement, had made no reference to his having found her on enclosed premises on which she was certainly trespassing, and she noted, too, that he had a word with the policeman on duty outside, before he walked to where he had left his car. Mrs Bradley waited for ten minutes, and then telephoned her Kensington house for carriers for the monkey and the parrot.

There were two immediate courses of action she could take, she thought. Both involved interviews with people she did not know. She remembered that David Harben had spoken to the next-door neighbour over the wall on the subject of weeds. It might well be that this apparently genial and simple-minded gentleman would have valuable information which he could be persuaded to share.

She went out into the garden and yodelled over the wall. Up came a head with the cautious enquiry of a tortoise.

'Good-day,' said Mrs Bradley. 'You remember, perhaps, a young man whom you helped in clearing weeds from this garden?'

'Ah, yes. The young fellow from the Sanitary Inspector's office. Said he kept a boat at moorings off here. I *said* I thought I knew his face.'

'Was that the last time you saw him?'

'Yes. Why, is anything the matter?'

'I want to get in touch with him.'

'Well, why don't you ring up the Sanitary Inspector?'

'Oh, yes, I could do that,' Mrs Bradley agreed. 'You don't happen to know whether his cousins have been here lately?'

'There *have* been people in and out, but I've taken no particular notice. I'm almost a newcomer to the district and I don't know people yet. I'm a bachelor, you see. A woman would know all about the neighbours by now, but – well, rightly or wrongly, I don't. Come over and have a look at my air-raid shelter.'

Mrs Bradley thanked him. There was no house on the other side for a distance of almost forty yards, and she did not feel that it would be of much use to extend the scope of her enquiries by visiting a house which, in town parlance, was scarcely that of a neighbour.

Instead, she decided to visit the almshouses. She had heard Harben speak of them, and believed that he had been accustomed to show the old men some little kindness when his boat was at moorings in their neighbourhood. Then another thought struck her. There was the public house not far from the almshouses, and Harben had turned in there for a drink before going on to the house – if to the house he had gone. She knew that Harben had met his friend Woods in this public house and that the message to her over the telephone had been agreed upon there.

It was just after two, and the little place was still open. It took less than five minutes to obtain the information she sought, and also to hear the name of the man who had telephoned, and to get some idea of his standing in the locality.

She went next to the six old men, but saw only five of them, for one was visiting his daughter. The little group of houses was built sideways on to the river, and a flagged pavement at right-angles to the concrete path led past all the front doors. Two of the pensioners were seated outside in the sun, so that it was easy enough to enter into conversation. These two brought out the others.

The old men were very ready to talk about Harben, but seemed to know nothing in particular about the inhabitants of the house.

'He were proper good,' said one old fellow, speaking of David. Another avowed that he was a gentleman.

'Many's the bottle of beer he've smuggled in here, to give us a treat, like,' said a third. The fourth remembered that he had been seen with a girl, but, so far as Mrs Bradley could make out from the description, it was not the girl from the house. The old man was over ninety and his memory was failing. Patiently she elicited all that he could tell her. She avoided putting leading questions, and correlated all that the old man said with what she already knew. She left presents of tobacco, and took with her the knowledge that she would be welcome ('baccy, or no baccy, mam,' said one old man) whenever she called again.

She went back to the house, and by half-past four a servant arrived with a cat-basket for the monkey and a screened cage for the parrot. At sight of the cage, the parrot observed sarcastically, 'Among the Otamys. Among the Otamys, old boy,' and bit Mrs Bradley's finger. The servant returned to Kensington with the pets, and Mrs Bradley to an anxious Sister Mary Dominic, to a consolatory Sister Mary Sebastian, and to a little group of unconsolable small boys.

'What, isn't he coming here any more?' asked one. 'Then who's going to take us fishing, like he said?'

'I'll take you myself,' said Mrs Bradley; but no one realized more fully than she did that this would not be the same thing.

She had noted, during her stay at the house by the river, the sage remarks of the parrot. It had spoken continuously of a dirty night at the *Cat's Whisker*, and also of Cripplegate, the latter in a negative sense, since it was 'not Cripplegate, old boy'.

Almost her first action was to write and rewrite the parrot's unusual remarks, first in one sequence and then in another, until she had six combinations. Then she put away her notebook, took out a volume of poetry and dismissed her guest and his affairs completely from her mind.

These tactics had their usual success. By the time she was in her tall, narrow London house on the following day, seated before a modest, cheerful fire and eating toast and drinking China tea (then still procurable) the problem had resolved itself to this:

The fact that the monkey and the parrot had been left in the house was no accident.

The monkey, which could be of no obvious use to her in tracing Harben and the girl, had probably been left to lull suspicion, since the parrot could be very useful indeed, and therefore it was invidious to draw too much attention to it.

If these premises were true, it followed that the girl, whatever her past deeds, might be friendly to Harben, wished to help him, and had left what clues she could on the parrot's raucous tongue to assist his friends to trace him.

The proper order of the parrot's remarks must be left to Fate to determine, since Mrs Bradley's subconscious mind had produced no indisputable sequence. One point, however, had emerged. Cripplegate inevitably suggested St Giles' Church. If it was *not* Cripplegate, a point on which the parrot seemed clear, it might be another St Giles'. This, taken together with the reference to Otamys and to the *Cat's Whisker*, seemed to suggest that a visit to St Giles'-in-the-Fields might be rewarded, since the *Cat's Whisker* was thieves' slang for a very differently named hostelry in the Soho area. She remembered, too, that Harben's winter quarters were in the Charing Cross Road. The word Otamys gave no trouble, for out of the back of her mind came a quotation from the *Beggar's Opera*: *'Poor Brother Tom had an Accident this time Twelvemonth, and so clever a made fellow he was, that I could not save him from those fleaing rascals the Surgeons; and now, poor Man, he is among the Otamys at Surgeons' Hall.'*

'Dear me!' murmured Mrs Bradley, upon acquiring this discouraging idea. 'I really do hope not, I must say.'

'Of course, I can see the point of you telling me this part of the yarn, ma'am, although, at first sight, it wouldn't seem to get us anywhere,' said Pirberry. 'You want to make clear, I take it, that Mr Harben was telling the truth some of the time. I suppose the tale about being hit over the head, and all that stuff about the dream and then waking up in an open boat and going to the

Canary Islands and bringing back those women, and so on, might have been partly true, too.'

'Or wholly true; or, of course, not true at all,' said Mrs Bradley. 'I'll emphasize one thing, though, Inspector. His account of his dream is very interesting, as I think I mentioned before.'

'All this psychology again, ma'am?'

'Yes.'

Pirberry's face fell. She laughed.

'The subconscious, ma'am?'

'Yes. But there's something more, something which *you* may find interesting.'

'Yes, ma'am?'

'To begin with, it's the sort of report of a dream that you would expect a novelist to make. Its craziness is nicely rounded off; the story is complete; there are no loose ends, as it were.'

'You mean he invented the dream, ma'am?'

'Not necessarily. He may believe he reported the dream as he dreamed it, although we ourselves, less accomplished story tellers, may feel quite certain that gaps have been filled in and situations filled out in a way that is hardly natural. But all that is by the way. One can make allowance for it. Lots of people embroider their dreams in the telling of them. They cannot bear an incomplete and pointless narrative. No; did you not gather that the dreamer was very pleased with himself over something? There is, to me, an immense amount of self satisfaction in that dream.'

'I can't see how that bears upon his disappearance, ma'am.'

'I don't know that it does bear upon his disappearance, Inspector, but it does indicate his state of mind, I think, and that state of mind should give us food for speculation if not for concrete ideas.'

'So you *don't* accept his story ma'am?' said Pirberry.

'I think he moved the body. I think he moved it not when he declared that it had gone, but rather later.'

'Why did the young lady run, ma'am, if the body was where she had left it?'

'It wasn't where she had left it. I believe what he says when he tells me that he placed it on the bed and covered the face. What does intrigue me, though, is the fact that the old man was poisoned. I don't think David poisoned him. In fact, it's pretty clear to me that David had no idea the old man had been poisoned, although I think perhaps the girl knew all the time.'

'The girl, then? You think she did it?'

'Possibly she did it. David was certain that she had committed the murder, I should say, but I am inclined to think that her flight indicates very strongly that *she* believed *him* guilty, and was afraid because of what he'd done.'

'But the note on the pennon?'

'Worded as he has stated, very likely. She did not want to get him into trouble. She distrusted her own discretion. Rightly, I feel. She has hardly shown herself discreet.'

'All surmise, ma'am, if I may say so.'

'All right,' said Mrs Bradley. 'You trace the arsenic, and if it isn't where I think it is, I'll give up all my theories.'

'You'll agree you're partial, ma'am?'

'Certainly I am, Inspector. I wonder whether you would try a little experiment?'

Pirberry looked at her dubiously.

'An experiment, ma'am?'

'A very simple one. Will you confront the next-door neighbour at the house by the river in Chiswick with the Spanish captain and Don Juan?'

'I will, if you say so, but why?'

'You'll know why when you've done it,' said Mrs Bradley. The experiment had a surprising result for Pirberry.

'He says he knows them, ma'am. He says they came several times to the house by the river during the old man's life-time. He says he always thought they were his sons. How one earth did you tumble to it, ma'am?'

'You'll know when I've finished the story; perhaps before then. But that is not all, Inspector. Take those stabbing affairs in Little Newport Street. El Piojo, poor, stupid fellow, really did take the blow intended for David. And, in the case of the captain, I think we shall find his brother, Don Juan, stabbed him, just as he said.'

'And the attack on *you*, ma'am?'

'Don Juan, again, I imagine. That is purely surmise. I didn't see him. The wretched little Italian was obviously innocent. I knew I'd tripped up the wrong man.'

'Then what do you think Mr Harben was up to, those months he reckoned he went to the Canary Islands?'

'I think he was taken on board a tug by the brothers, and may have been cast adrift off the Spanish coast. There is no doubt that the captain and Don Juan are really seamen, and the others form part of their crew. The captain and Don Juan may be the old man's sons, but I think they are Leda's brothers. They are if the Bible and book of poems were hers. I think they knew that their sister had made an unhappy marriage. In addition, they may have thought they would gain by the old man's death. I think they came to England (before the war, you see) and stayed at the old man's house. If that is so, they are almost as suspect as Harben. Leda went out, possibly, and must have come back to find her husband dead. She went to Harben, certain, I suppose, that he had done the deed. He must often have wished the old man dead, of course.

'I don't see how you think they were brothers, ma'am, nor how the lady comes to be their sister.'

'The mate's name was Juan Hueza. The name on the books was Inez Hueza, as I told you. The captain said Don Juan was his sister's husband's brother-in-law. Work that out.'

'Ah,' said Pirberry. 'Well, wouldn't she have suspected her brothers, sooner than Mr Harben?'

'Most likely she believed they'd gone to sea again. They'd have let her understand that if they'd planned the murder.'

## CHAPTER SIXTEEN

# *Muddy Beer*

The *Cat's Whisker* was, at any rate, a starting-point, and a significant one, at that, Mrs Bradley thought. Next morning she went to Leicester Square by Tube, and commenced a survey of the district. At the police station in Charing Cross Road she almost knocked into an acquaintance of hers who was coming down the steps. They greeted one another warmly.

'And what are you doing so far from your home, Mr Pirberry?' enquired Mrs Bradley.

Detective-Inspector Pirberry, of the Criminal Investigation Department, shrewdly replied:

'About the same as you, ma'am, I shouldn't wonder. Sir Beresford tipped me off about this Mr Harben who's missing from your house. Besides, we got a tip to keep an eye on the *Cat's Whisker*. I presume you know where that is, ma'am? Although that's not its real name?'

'I know well enough,' Mrs Bradley replied. 'It's very curious, I must say. Very curious indeed.'

'How so, ma'am, if I may ask?'

Mrs Bradley aptly quoted the parrot as they walked towards the Strand. The detective-inspector was on his way back to New Scotland Yard, and she had her own reasons for wishing to view the river from the nearest point to Saint Giles' in the Fields.

They parted at the riverside end of Craven Street, Pirberry to go westward along the Embankment, Mrs Bradley to cross the road and stand for some time by Charing Cross Pier before she began to walk down-river. She passed the obelisk of Cleopatra's Needle, crossed the road again, this time to walk up Norfolk Street, crossed the Strand, and so, by way of Bow Street and across Long Acre, went to Endell Street. Coming thence into Broad Street she was struck by a slight coincidence. Broad Street was hard by Saint Giles' High Street, just as, in Oxford City,

Saint Giles' and Broad Street were near neighbours. She did not imagine that the connection would help her to find Harben, but she filed the fact in her mind for future reference, and took her way from Broad Street into Maidenhead Close with the intention of going into New Oxford Street for a taxi to take her back to Kensington.

Half-way along one side of Maidenhead Close, however, she came upon what, at first sight, seemed an extraordinary building. She was so much fascinated by its appearance that she stopped to look at it.

The building was certainly unique and she had to traverse two sides of a square in order to appreciate all it had (from the outside, at least) to show.

At some time during the mid-nineteenth century a Baptist chapel of impressive dimensions and in the neo-Ruskin style of Byzantine architecture had been erected in this most cosmopolitan district of London, out of money subscribed by a pious publican. As time went on, the trustees of the chapel had felt the need for a church parlour, a recreation room for their young men, another for trustees' meetings, a larger room for chapel teas, rooms in which week-day Bible classes could be held – in short, the trustees found the need for another whole building in addition to the place of worship.

Unfortunately, extra ground was unobtainable by the time the plan was fully formulated, but a happy compromise had been achieved by the addition to the existing building of an upper floor with a separate entrance and a staircase. A lift had been installed at a still later date, and Mrs Bradley's first view had been of the back door of these premises. There was nothing very much to suggest a church or chapel in what she saw. It was not until she had walked round to the front that she could discover the true function of the building.

She returned to Maidenhead Close, and, watched by a couple of slatternly women who had appeared from an alley which opened out of the opposite side of the thoroughfare, she looked again at the small doorway which opened on to a flight of stone steps leading up by the side of the lift-shaft. Another set of steps led down to some subterranean cavern below the level of the street. There was another entrance – or, rather, exit, she discovered – near the main entrance to the chapel. This was closed. Further along Maidenhead Close itself there was a flight of very narrow outside steps which led to a very small opening in the wall. It seemed as though these outside steps must lead to a furnace-room or a coal store, for there was coal dust all the way up them. They were made secure by an iron railing, were not only narrow but shallow, and exercised upon her the strange fascination which flights of steps have for children, stray cats and some painters.

She looked for some time at the building before resuming her walk, and, on the way home, amused herself by making plans in her notebook of the original structure and then made the additions to it.

'You got to know it better later on, ma'am,' Pirberry suggested. She agreed, and added:

'Curious I should have noticed it at all.'

'Oh, I don't know. It's very historic round there, ma'am.'

'It will, at all events, take its place in the annals of crime,' said Mrs Bradley.

Curiously enough, she was involved, through the agency of some relatives by marriage who lived on the outskirts of a town called Willington near the ancient city of Winborough, in a series of murders which took place during those first autumn months of the war. As it seemed likely that her niece might be involved (although only as a witness at the trial) she felt she could not disregard her family obligations, the more so as there seemed no clue to Harben's disappearance. So she was obliged to leave, for a time, in the hands of the police, the curious affair she was investigating, and devote her talents to the interests of her relatives.

By the end of the year, however, she was free of Willington, and was able to exercise her time once again as she chose. Her choice was to address herself afresh to the problem of Harben's disappearance.

Her cook, a temperamental Frenchman, had been bitten twice by the monkey, and the parrot now confined itself to the expression, 'Muddy beer!' This it was wont to repeat at five-second intervals when in the mood for conversation, and the household were becoming tired of it. Mrs Bradley reminded it of its previous, more extensive vocabulary, but with no success whatsoever.

One evening in the following March, about a week before Harben got home from his curious little Odyssey, she was called into consultation by the War Office which required the services of a psychiatrist for some special work.

Sighing (for she disliked commissions of this sort, which were usually rather uninteresting and not, in her opinion, particularly useful), Mrs Bradley answered the letter, sent it, with other letters, to the post, and had just settled down to talk to the parrot which had been brought into the study by her orders, when the telephone rang.

'Traced that empty cistern. Remember it, ma'am?' said Detective-Inspector Pirberry's voice, speaking cheerfully. 'Came from another house in Chiswick. All quite local, you see.'

'Does it help us?' Mrs Bradley enquired.

'Too soon to tell. There are some pretty good prints, of course, but there's very little chance the top ones will turn out to be those of the previous owners. We're on their trail now. At least, the locals are. Don't suppose they'll have much trouble finding them, that's one thing. Probably evacuated when the war began.'

He rang off. Mrs Bradley went back to the fireside and the parrot.

'Otamys,' she said, giving it a lump of sugar. 'Otamys, old boy, old boy.'

The parrot cocked his head at her, but did not repeat the sentence.

'Not Cripplegate,' she continued. 'Not Cripplegate. Not Cripplegate.'

The parrot cocked his head again. She tried him with the name of the public house, but again he did not respond.

'Muddy beer!' said Mrs Bradley sadly. He did perk up at this, and said it for her half a dozen times in succession. They were friendly now. He never attacked her fingers, nor danced on his perch, nor swayed himself to and fro when she approached. She decided upon an experiment. Fetching a green baize cloth, she put it over the cage, carried the cage to a neighbouring taxi rank, got into a cab, and directed the driver to go to the Tube Station at Leicester Square.

Here she got out, and, having walked, by way of the Charing Cross Road, as far as the *Cat's Whisker*, she went inside with the parrot, left the baize on the cage, placed the cage on one of the tables, and then went up to the counter.

The *Cat's Whisker* was well disguised as a reputable tavern. It had, of course, another name besides the sobriquet bestowed on it by its habituees and the police. She went unremarked by the customers, except for a civil exchange of dignified greetings. The barman, a grey-headed man of sixty, was swabbing down the bar counter, and said cheerily:

'Evening, ma! And what's yours?'

'Rum,' said Mrs Bradley, mentioning the first drink which came into her head.

She did not uncover the parrot's cage that night, although she noticed the interested glances cast at it by some of the customers. These were of all kinds, and, for the most part, were men. There were merchant seamen, some naval ratings, soldiers and Royal Air Force, but most of the 'regulars' were civilians and of all nationalities – naturalized, she supposed.

The place was orderly and quiet, but a great many surreptitious conferences seemed to take place at the bar, and the place was divided, it seemed to her, very sharply into regular customers and casuals. The latter did not seem to stay long. The atmosphere, although cordial up to a point, was never friendly towards them, and none of them seemed inclined to prolong his stay. Most, from what she could overhear, proposed to seek somewhere livelier, but the real reason for their departure, whether they knew it or not, was that there was something discouraging in the air, as though those who knew the place and had, in a sense, the freedom of it, were holding back until the unwanted casuals were gone.

Mrs Bradley held her ground longer than most, and would have stayed longer still, but that she did not want to become an object of annoyance or suspicion. She had a second double rum, which she made to last as long as ever she could – it was, to say the least, a very fine rum she was drinking – and then she left.

She went twice a week, after that, and began to be regarded as little as though she were part of the furnishings. The barman, in fact, became her admirer, and would give her the straight tip about what he had deduced was her trade.

'Evening, ma! Same as usual?'

'Good evening, Bartlemas. Same as usual, please. And how's the market?'

'Better for you today, ma. Best prices for piano-accordions, babies' prams, pictures painted on rough glass, and the usual rude books.'

'Thank you, Bartlemas. That ought to suit me nicely.'

'And if you *should* get a few fur coats, ma, just you hang on to 'em like glue. Don't you let none of them Yid fanciers go doing you down. Fur coats is going to nicey-pricey about the third year of the war. You stick the moth-balls in 'em, ma, and pack 'em in lavender. Be able to retire on 'em, you will.'

'Thank you, Bartlemas,' said Mrs Bradley gratefully.

It had become the barman's firm conviction that anybody as respectable as Mrs Bradley must be a receiver of stolen goods, and one in a fair way of business, and as to be labelled criminal, in some form or another, at the *Cat's Whisker* was a passport to favour, Mrs Bradley had never denied the soft impeachment of being a female fence. Besides, in her view, it was preferable to be thought a receiver than to be suspected of some of the vicious occupations which flourished (and had done for three hundred years) between the purlieus of Charing Cross Road and the environs of Drury Lane.

'Nice bird you got there,' went on the barman, polishing tumblers but sparing an eye for the parrot and its brightly gilded cage. She always took it with her and sometimes took the green baize cloth off.

'Yes. Let's drink its health,' said Mrs Bradley. 'Have one on me. No, make it a double. I've done pretty well today.' The barman said he was glad of that, and added, 'Can't say the same meself. Now take my boy. Only out of Pentonville Saturday, and goes and joins the Army today. Silly fellow, I says. Miss all his chances, he will. Why, if we get a bit of bombing over here' – he lowered his voice – 'there'll be pickings to have for the picking up, so to say. And all these evacuated people! And Specials in place of the Regulars! Why, it's throwing his money down a drain, to go off and join the Army now!'

Just as he finished this Jeremiad, two customers came in. They were dark-faced men in reefer jackets and merchant seamen's caps, and one wore ear-rings. Slapping down money on the counter, this one said:

'Double Scotch twice. Where's the soda?'

'Where do you think it is?' asked Bartlemas, mildly. 'Where would you expect it to be? Right at your elbow, ain't it?'

'None of your lip,' said the man. Mrs Bradley had never seen the two before. The man took the drinks over to a table next but one to that occupied by Mrs Bradley's parrot. His companion joined him, and, putting their heads close together, the two began to talk in low tones as they sipped their drinks. The parrot, suddenly bored by its drab surroundings, bit the wires of the cage with some ferocity, scrabbled its claws on the perch, and suddenly shouted:

'Muddy beer! Muddy beer, by cripes!'

The effect of this on the whisky-drinking couple was remarkable. The man with the ear-rings gave such a start that his elbow caught his companion's glass and it would have gone over but for the jugglery of its owner, who fielded it in a flash and carried it to his lips before its precious contents could suffer any fate but the one he had decreed for them. He swallowed, coughed, and got up.

'That bird!' said the other, who had already risen to his feet and was pointing at the cage. 'How come you got a bird what says "Muddy beer"?'

'How come you get rubbering why the lady's boid says "Muddy beer", you big sap?' enquired his companion, morosely. 'Come on! Step on it!' At this, they left the bar, the smaller man retaining sufficient presence of mind to swipe the contents of his comrade's glass before running to join him in the doorway.

'Well! well!' said Mrs Bradley, when the swing door had closed behind them. 'Peculiar people!'

'You said it,' said the barman, nodding.

'Not Cripplegate, not Cripplegate, not Cripplegate, old boy, old boy, old boy!' shrieked the parrot, which seemed to have recovered its form and the whole of its répertoire in a night.

Mrs Bradley put the green baize over it. She remained in the bar for an hour and a half, and then made her way home by taxi, having left the parrot with Bartlemas 'in trust', as she solemnly informed him, and her hat, rather less ostentatiously, under one of the tables.

Bartlemas, who was accustomed to queer presents and queerer clients, accepted the parrot without demur.

'Though if he turns out unlucky and drives custom away, like what he done tonight, I'll wring his neck,' he said. 'But I reckon he'll be an attraction.' Mrs Bradley said she hoped that this would prove to be the case, and, disregarding Sherlock Holmes' advice about cabs, took the first taxi that came up and returned to Kensington. From her house she telephoned Detective-Inspector Pirberry, and gave him a painstaking description of the two men who had left the Cat's Whisker so hastily.

'There are more ways of starting a hare than are put down in Police Regulations, ma'am,' said Pirberry, laughing.

'The same applies to wild geese,' said Mrs Bradley. 'Tomorrow I try St Giles' High Street again, and re-read the tablets in the church. If I see our two sailors on my way, I'll let you know.'

'Just as you say, ma'am. But no doubt we shall pull them in.'

He did pull them in. Mrs Bradley received a telephone call in the morning to request her to come to Vine Street and identify them.

'So you was just a nark, lady,' said the man with the Cockney accent and the ear-rings.

'Rubbering round,' said his companion. 'Giving us the woiks,' he added sorrowfully.

'And now *I* carry on,' said Pirberry. 'Who are you working with, Beetler?'

'Going straight, straight I am,' said Ear-rings. 'Merchant navy. Prove it to you if I had my papers here.'

'No doubt. And what's all this about muddy beer? And who

carried a bloke out of a house on the river near Chiswick? Carried him out, what's more, in an empty cistern? Who croaked him? Come on; talk.'

'He wasn't croaked, governor, was he? We never intended that! I never touched him. That was the skipper, I reckon. Must have been. Said he was canned, and had got to be tooken home. That's all I know. Straight it is, Mr Pirberry!'

'What about you, Kidnapper?' asked Pirberry pleasantly. The smaller man jerked his head, a gesture implying, it seemed, resignation combined with a kind of sad self-justification.

'What he says goes,' he replied. 'We fetch up at the joint and get our orders. Well, we carry 'em out. Ain't that what orders is for? Then we beat it, like we been told. Anything wrong about that?'

'You'll see,' replied Pirberry. 'Well, come on. I can't wait here all day. Where do I find this skipper?'

'Search me,' said Ear-rings, curtly. 'All we knows is he gets our name and address from Plug Williams — you know Plug — keeps a little sports shop in Mild Close, on the corner – '

'I know Plug. All right, buddies. Off you go, and the less said the better. Understand?'

'Sure,' they said; and slouched out. Pirberry scratched his head.

'Don't know whether I'm doing the best thing in letting them go like that, but there's nothing on which we can hold them. You can't jug a man for leaving a public house before he's finished his drink. Of course, their finger-prints are on that cistern, as I daresay you gathered, ma'am. But I rushed 'em as far as I think I'd better, about that, at any rate for a bit. Now there's Plug Williams to see. I wonder how far these boys will tip him off before I get there?'

'Is the name Plug derived from tobacco habits or from his boxing?' Mrs Bradley enquired.

'A bit of both, I believe, ma'am. But somehow I don't believe we've got hold of the right stick – let alone the right end of it. I don't see those boys as murderers. There's something behind their statement.'

'It isn't like you to be pessimistic, Mr Pirberry,' said Mrs

Bradley, studying him thoughtfully. 'Never mind! Let's go and see Plug.'

Mrs Bradley grinned reminiscently.

'You will remember our abortive visit?' she observed.

'Very well, ma'am. But I never knew what you were up to. I never knew you had a thought beyond Mr Harben's disappearance. You shouldn't have kept me in the dark, ma'am, about the old man's death.'

'And yet, Inspector, what could I do? Mr Harben had confided in me – and there was, after all, no body.'

Pirberry looked at her, and shook his head.

'Sophistry?' said Mrs Bradley, grinning. 'Well, perhaps it is. But I got what I wanted out of Plug.'

'You did, ma'am. More than I managed to do!'

'You were working in the dark, in a sense. It was hardly fair. But now we have found the corpse . . .'

'Not *the* corpse. *A* corpse, ma'am, until we get it identified for certain.'

'Thank you. Now that we have found an unaccountable, interesting, significant, magnificently dressing-gowned corpse in a box which would fit the marks left on the lawn of the house by the river . . .'

Pirberry grinned, and gave in.

## CHAPTER SEVENTEEN

### *Welshman*

Plug Williams retained the Glamorgan cadence of his youth. He was a short, broad, round-headed, fiery little man with the manners of a local preacher and the morals (according to Pirberry) of a pimp. For a short time he had been a merchant seaman, and bore proudly upon his chest the badge called the Prince of Wales' feathers. In place of the usual motto, the tattooist had added 'Me too', with all the appropriate emphasis of a heavy Gothic script.

Pirberry and Mrs Bradley found Plug at home in the room behind his shop. He was playing draughts with a friend. The shop, which was rather optimistically labelled *The Sports Store*, offered a couple of greenheart fishing rods, some haversacks of an inexpensive kind, one pair of football boots, sets of darts, cheap but innocuous literature, various embrocations and liniments in bottles, a fly-whisk, studs for football boots, a chest-developer, two sets of boxing gloves, a bottle of cough sweets, boot laces, jock straps, a cricket belt with a snake buckle, several technical works all priced at one and sixpence and dealing with the various forms of sport, a landing net, a table-tennis set in a box, dominoes, dice, half a dozen electric torches, two lanyards, some boxes of corn-cure and a tin of air-gun pellets.

Finding no one in the shop, Pirberry banged on the counter, and the proprietor came out of the back room like a crab turned dancing master.

'No neet to make a noise,' he observed austerely.

Pirberry disclosed his identity. Mrs Bradley, who had remained in the background, found herself subjected to the scrutiny, swift, but, she felt, complete, of a pair of small, suspicious but not unfriendly eyes.

'Plug Williams?' asked Pirberry.

'Indeed yes.'

'Well, Mr Williams, we've been sent to you by a couple of chaps named Beetler Hankin and Kidnapper Brent, sailors. Know them?'

'Indeed, yes. Why not, then?'

'No "why not" about it. What about muddy beer?'

The Welshman stared at him in perplexity.

'You are choking, isn't it?' he said.

'I don't think so,' said Pirberry, putting a finger to his collar.

'Joking,' murmured Mrs Bradley's voice behind him.

'Oh, ah, yes. No,' he added, addressing Williams again. 'No, I'm not joking. Let's try again, Mr Williams. You were good enough, some time ago, to put a ship's captain on to Hankin and Brent. When would that have been?'

Plug appeared to search his memory. Apparently it failed him. He shook his round head, pursed up his little fat lips, and then shook his head once more.

'Come on!' said Pirberry impatiently. 'You know me, for all you pretended you didn't. I haven't got all day to muck about. What's St Giles'-in-the-Fields got to do with it?'

'Sir,' said Mr Williams, with great dignity 'to assist the police I am willing always, isn't it? Indeed to God yes,' he added, reassuring himself on this point. 'But innocent I am of all complicity in crime.'

'Who's talking about crime?' demanded Pirberry. Plug picked up an open box of darts from the counter, looked inside it, clicked his tongue, turned to the shelf behind him, took up a small tin of metal polish and a blackened cloth, and set to work to clean off a speck of rust on one of the darts.

'Me, that is. Thorough, so I am,' he observed. These irritating tactics had their effect on Pirberry. He turned and marched out of the shop, saying over his shoulder:

'You're playing a mug's game, Plug. There's more behind this than you might think.'

'And what more?' Williams enquired.

'Murder,' said Pirberry briefly; and walked out.

'Now, wouldn't you call that an impatient, unreasonable man?' said Williams, subjecting the dart to one last scrutiny before he replaced it in the box. He screwed the top on the tin of metal polish, put it back in its place, gave the cloth a slight flick, laid it down, and then looked at Mrs Bradley as though surprised to see her standing there.

'Wass you not with the policeman bach?' he enquired.

'Does it look like it?' Mrs Bradley asked. 'I want to see your gymnasium,' she added, smiling. The smile appeared to fascinate Mr Williams.

'What is that you are saying?' he enquired.

'Your gymnasium,' repeated Mrs Bradley. 'You *have* a gymnasium, haven't you? They told me at the Baths they thought you had.'

She had heard a disciplined scuffling overhead when first she had entered the shop.

'Come up you,' said Mr Williams, much more cordially. 'Tuition in boxing, was it, for a nephew or son, perhaps?'

'Grandson,' said Mrs Bradley. 'His grandfather is nervous, but I think a boy needs a manly sport.'

She followed the proprietor through a door at the back, and found in the room a sallow-faced man in a suit of overalls seated patiently in front of a draught-board.

'Sorry I am, Sunny Boy,' said Mr Williams. 'But business I have, as you see.'

The sallow man waved aside the apology, and, picking up one of the pieces which he had captured during the game, attempted to balance it on the end of one finger. Mr Williams led the way upstairs.

'In the game I was, yes, indeed, until too old I am,' he explained, as he opened a baize-covered door at the top. 'Go in first, I will, if you please, to see that the boys are dressed for a woman to see. Not often ladies we have.'

He closed the door behind himself, but appeared in less than five seconds.

'All right they are. Just resting. In their gowns.'

The resting youths were obviously of Jewish extraction. Clad in faded dressing-gowns, presumably the property of Williams, since each was embroidered on the back with his name in full, they were leaning on the parallel bars at the side of the room, chewing gum and exchanging information about greyhounds.

The room was a very large one. A twenty-foot space marked off with thick white lines was the boxing ring, and, besides this and the parallel bars, the room contained a punching ball on a stand clamped down to the floor, a table for massage and another for billiards.

'All over my two rooms below it goes, and over my place at the back,' explained Williams, going to one of the windows and looking out. 'Your grandson would be how old? Sixteen, then?'

'Seventeen, and weighs just over ten stone?'

'Ah, ten stone is it? Nice that is. Come here, Bennie bach, and show me that left hook. Slow you are with it, slow; and that iss the death of the game, and a dirty death, wasn't it, at that?'

One of the youths came forward, dropping his dressing-gown

on the floor. He sparred with Williams for a minute or two, then Williams thrust him away and told him to dress.

'You would like to pay twelve and six a lesson?' he enquired of Mrs Bradley. She shook her head.

'How much do these boys pay?' she pertinently enquired.

'Well, now, indeed, they'll be professionals, look you,' said Williams earnestly. 'I shall get a nice picking off them when I get them into the game. I'll manage for them, see? And get a percentage, see? My living they are, these boys. Chews they are, you see. They'll get on to the money, Chews will.'

'I can't pay more than seven and sixpence a lesson,' said Mrs Bradley firmly. The Welshman shook his head.

'I don't want private pupils, look you,' he pointed out. 'A great waste of my time it is. Go, you, and see what your old man have to say.'

Scarcely had they got back into the shop when Pirberry re-entered it from the street.

'What was the name of the skipper?' he demanded.

'Toms, Inspector bach,' replied the Welshman, without a second's thought. 'And the boys are taking the rap for him, so they are. Good boys, well-paid, they are.'

'Where does he live?'

'I wouldn't know, would I? Be a reasonable man, now.'

'Where did you meet him?'

'On a ship, the *Countersign*, of London. He was the captain, and saved my life when I was poisoned with some bad shell-fish in Naples one time. All had given me up, but not the skipper. A fine fellow he was, and when he comes here looking for two good fellows for a bit of work he has for them to do, why, look you, I recommended to him those boys. Good boys they are, and strong boys. Yes, indeed. And not afraid to take the rap for anyone, because they know they can clear themselves. See? They are very well satisfied, too, with what he gives them. Very well satisfied they are.'

'They'll be a lot less satisfied by the time I've done with them,' said Pirberry. 'And you can tell them so when you see them. They'll be lucky if they don't get fourteen years for being accessories, you know.'

'Dear, dear!' said Williams, nodding his head. 'Yes, indeed! Misguided they are, but good-hearted. They are like the police, isn't it? They would help anyone in trouble.'

He picked up a second dart from the open box upon the counter, scrutinized its metal shaft, and reached for his blackened cloth and his little tin of polish, avoiding Pirberry's eye, but conveying to an unprejudiced observer the impression of an industrious, virtuous man.

Pirberry snorted.

'Please yourself, Plug,' he observed. 'I wonder whether you've met a Mr Harben, lives round these parts every winter?'

'David Harben?' said Williams, interested. 'And what nicer boy could you wish to meet than David?'

'The trouble is, it's no use wishing to meet him,' said Pirberry sourly. 'Somebody's done for Harben, and somebody's going to swing.'

'Well, well,' said Williams, philosophically.

'And there's a very great rascal,' said Pirberry, when Mrs Bradley rejoined him in Cambridge Circus just outside the Palace Theatre. 'What did you stay for, ma'am?'

'Nothing very much,' said Mrs Bradley. 'I didn't particularly want him to connect us, so I remained to discuss with him his terms for teaching my grandson to box. I suppose you can find me a young policeman or someone?'

'Yes, there's a Flying Squad fellow you can have – somebody Plug won't know. No use sending him one of the fellows from the Charing Cross Road or Gray's Inn Road stations. He's certain to know all of those. Why, what's the idea?'

'Just to leave with Mr Williams a picker-up of unconsidered trifles.'

'And not a bad idea, either. I could do with a line on Plug myself, and that's much the best way to set about it. A brainy notion, ma'am, if I may say so.'

'I've beaten Plug down to nine and sixpence,' said Mrs Bradley complacently. 'He doesn't want pupils, he tells me. I don't know whether the boy we send will learn much, except how to box.'

'He'll learn that all right,' said Pirberry. 'Another thing about

Plug; he's a judo expert. Lots of people don't know that, but a fellow I had a tussle with once, who threw me over a backyard fence in Pimlico, told me afterwards, when we'd pinched him – it took four of us, I might tell you – that he learned his stuff from Plug Williams.'

'That's interesting,' said Mrs Bradley slowly. 'I saw the gymnasium, of course.' She described it.

Pirberry nodded.

'Sounds above-board, all right, but we happen to know he isn't. What are you going to do now?'

'I'm going to find Captain Toms.'

'Don't bother, ma'am. That's our job. We've got the machinery for it. Now we've learnt the name of that ship we shall be all right.'

'I doubt it,' said Mrs Bradley. 'Do you know the kind of ship she is?'

'No, but she'll be registered at Lloyds. It only means looking up her record.'

'Well, good luck,' said Mrs Bradley, 'but I think I'd like to dabble, just the same.'

'Suit yourself, ma'am,' said Pirberry, knowing that she would do this in any case.

She did not, however, attempt to emulate the tactics of the police, but sat down and collected in a methodical, logical manner such evidence as she had garnered.

Broadly observed, it smelt of the sea. There was the parrot, often a link with sailors. There was the disappearance of a man known to be an amateur yachtsman. There were the seafaring men Hankin and Brent who had been employed by the (so far) mysterious and unreal Captain Toms. There was the ex-pugilist, ex-sailor Williams, who seemed to be the connecting link between the captain and the merchant seamen. Lastly, there was the ship which had been mentioned – the *Countersign*. Was it her imagination, or was there something unusual about this name? Ships' names seemed inevitable, somehow. The ships of literature and history – the *Golden Hind, Saucy Hispaniola, Mayflower, Speedwell, Harry Grace à Dieu, Moonraker, Bounty, Santa Maria, Argo, Victory* – these all had right-sounding names.

*Countersign* should be in the same tradition, but it was not. It did not sound like a ship. But at that she had to leave it.

A point of real interest soon emerged, however. The *Countersign* was not in Lloyds' lists. Pirberry telephoned her a week later, and reported the total failure of the police, or of Lloyds' agents in London to account for any ship called *Countersign*.

'Dear, dear!' said Mrs Bradley, over the wire. 'And what are you going to do now?'

'Going to try and bounce something more out of Williams. We shan't do it, ma'am,' was his weak and dispirited reply. 'Not until Mr Harben's body turns up.'

'Come, come!' said Mrs Bradley. 'Don't despair!'

'So you never believed for a minute that Mr Harben was dead, ma'am?' Pirberry observed.

'Well, I liked him, you know,' said Mrs Bradley, 'and one hates to think that one's friends have been murdered, don't you think?'

Pirberry eyed her warily, but she remained perfectly grave.

'It was about then that I had another interview with Sir Beresford at the Yard,' he said, changing the subject. 'His view was that Mr Harben had disappeared for reasons known only to himself, and had taken the lady with him.'

'It was a reasonable surmise,' Mrs Bradley admitted. 'In fact, if we do not accept Mr Harben's own story of his disappearance, we ourselves might agree with Sir Beresford. One more thing I did at about that time. I looked up the local directory. The name of the owner of the house was Emmanuel Sandys, so that did not help the enquiry. I checked it with local tradespeople to make quite sure that that was the name on their books.'

'And, of course, it was,' said Pirberry. 'And that makes another dead end, ma'am.'

'There is one more interesting thing about that cistern,' said Mrs Bradley. 'What do you make of these prints?'

Pirberry studied two photographs.

'Identical, ma'am, I should say. I'd have to let our experts look at them to make certain, but they seem identical to me.'

'And to me,' she agreed complacently. 'One set were taken by your experts from those superimposed on others upon that empty cistern, and the other set are David Harben's from his tooth-glass.'

Pirberry looked at her in perplexity.

'I can't make you out, ma'am,' he said. 'One minute you believe in his innocence and swear by him, and the next you're presenting me with direct evidence of his guilt.'

'I told you I thought David helped to move the old man's body. It seems fairly certain that he is the Captain Toms referred to by Mr Williams, and that Hankin and Brent assisted him in carrying the cistern to the river. Of course, I never did think that David and the girl went back to the house as soon as he says they did. For one thing, he would have had to make certain that *rigor mortis* had passed off before he could get the body into the cistern.'

'What becomes of your water-gate theory, ma'am?'

'I don't know that it was ever a theory, Inspector. And I did not then know Hankin and Brent, nor their sensitiveness to the conversation of the parrot. Incidentally, that is not the only thing. In the interval between the disappearance and reappearance of David, there was an attempt . . .'

## CHAPTER EIGHTEEN

# Angels

Mrs Bradley pondered long upon Plug Williams and his half truths, upon the self-sacrificing seamen Beetler Hankin and Kidnapper Brent and upon their nervous reactions in taking to their heels at the *Cat's Whisker* at the sound of the parrot's 'Muddy beer'.

She went to Saint Giles'-in-the-Fields, pushed open its heavy iron gate, mounted to the plinth before the door, looked at the neatly tilled ground between the bushes, speculated on the possibilities of the old man's body having been interred there privately by Harben.

The church, on the Saturday afternoon that she visited it, was locked, and the neighbourhood was almost deserted. Occasionally someone would pass from narrow street into narrower alley, but none seemed to take the slightest notice of her as she loitered on the steps and gazed at the trim church garden.

'It might be possible,' she thought; but if the body had been there, in whose interest would it have been to draw attention to Saint Giles' by teaching a sentence to the parrot? And who was responsible, anyway, for the parrot's peculiar répertoire? That was a fundamental point, she felt, if one wanted to solve the mystery of David's disappearance.

She decided to return to Helsey Marsh and lay some of her findings, if not perhaps quite all, before the keen minds and hair splitting intelligences of Sister Mary Sebastian and Sister Mary Dominic.

'We have been quite worried about you,' they said. They asked for news of David, but Mrs Bradley was obliged to confess her utter failure to obtain any news of him at all.

'But I want your help and sympathetic counsel,' she said. So, when the hour which they allowed themselves for recreation came, the white-robed sisters took chairs on either side of the hearth in Mrs Bradley's cheerful dining-room, settled themselves with their mending – the boys' shirts and socks, mostly – and listened very attentively to the following sentences, which, read aloud in Mrs Bradley's deep and golden voice, sounded considerably more impressive than they were.

'Holborn means a brook in a hollow,' read Mrs Bradley.

'In Oxford, St Giles' abuts on to Broad Street; so in London.

'Soho is thought by some antiquarians to have obtained this curious name because hunting used to be carried on there, a theory suggested also by the "Dog and Duck" Tavern.

'Dyott Street was originally named Maidenhead Close; later, George Street. It received its present name from a family which flourished in the neighbourhood during the Stuart Period.

'High Holborn formed part of the route along which condemned criminals passed from Newgate Prison to Tyburn. The great bell of St Giles' was tolled when the condemned man was passing.

'Matilda, the Queen of King Henry I, founded a hospital for lepers near the site of the present church of St Giles'-in-the-Fields. Later, a manor house stood there, and its grounds included the land across which Denmark Street, Little Denmark Street and part of Charing Cross Road now run.

'The poet Dryden died in Gerrard Street, and the essayist de Quincey, when he was seated on a doorstep in Soho Square, was befriended by a street-walker.

'John Wright, an oilman (shopkeeper) of Compton Street, paid the funeral expenses of the King of Corsica in the early nineteenth century.'

She laid aside her notebook, looked at the two bent heads, cackled suddenly, and then, as though she were presenting a corollary to her reading, she referred to the curious effect on the sailors of the parrot's remark; of the fact that the ship mentioned by Williams could not be traced; and referred to the point that every bit of information she had gathered seemed to turn on the sea and on sailors.

'And now, my dear children, make something reasonable for me out of all that,' she commanded. Sister Mary Sebastian looked up with her usual happy expression.

'But it's all such a muddle, dear Mrs Bradley,' she said. Sister Mary Dominic looked troubled.

'He would not have caused all this worry and anxiety if he could have helped it,' she said. She folded her work and put it away in the large cardboard box which Mrs Bradley's manservant had found for her. She put the box in its corner, ready for next day's recreation time, folded her hands in her sleeves, and bowed to the two older women. At the door she turned round.

'I shall think about what you have said. If there is any virtue in it at all, then God will show it,' she said. They could hear her quiet footfalls on the stairs.

'She will pray. I shall pray,' said Sister Mary Sebastian. 'You have done all you can. The rest is with God. We shall find him.'

Mrs Bradley, who was not accustomed to regard God as a master detective, was considerably impressed by their attitude. She was not optimistic, however. She thought, as Pirberry thought, that there might be something more which Plug

Williams could tell if he would. She also agreed with Pirberry that the chances of his consenting to tell it – at any rate to the police – were indeed slender.

She went to bed at midnight with no plans for the morrow, and almost immediately slept.

She was not often troubled by dreams – not, at any rate, sufficiently so to remember the dreams in the morning – but on this particular night she did dream. She dreamt that she was in Norway, and that a cold wind blowing from the mountains brought to her ears the sounds of someone crawling down the mountainside towards her. Suddenly there was a crash, as a great boulder detached itself from a cliff and fell on to a river of ice at the foot of the mountain.

The noise woke her. She sat up, wide-eyed and alert; not in the least alarmed (for that was not her nature) but aware that the noise, although her dreaming ear had exaggerated it and had transposed it to something with which the dream-sequence could fit in, was a real noise. Her waking brain diagnosed it immediately as the crash of a closing door.

She reached out for the bed-head switch, but remembered in time that the strong draught blowing from the window might mean that the room was no longer completely blacked out. She reached for her torch, and switched it on. Then she heard the voice of Sister Mary Dominic at the window.

'It's all right. I think he's gone.'

'Who was it?' Mrs Bradley enquired. She heard the sound of the window-catch and the twitch of the curtain, reached out for her dressing-gown, and then switched on the light.

'I've closed the window,' said Sister Mary Dominic.

'Ah, yes! The cold wind from the mountains,' said Mrs Bradley. 'And now, dear child, how do you come to be up and dressed at two o'clock in the morning? Come into the dining-room. Perhaps we can stoke up the fire, and then you can tell me what has happened.'

With the aid of a couple of sticks she stimulated the dining-room fire to a respectable semblance of itself, produced sherry and biscuits, and waved her young guest to a chair. Sister Mary

Dominic refused the refreshment, sat upright, smoothed her scapula, folded her hands and proceeded to tell her story.

'I went into the garden to pray. It was cold, but there were stars. I am accustomed in Lent to make night prayers. I heard the men at the gate. I did not like the sound of their voices. I do not think they saw me because the willow hedge was between us. They moved towards the house. I heard them climbing up. I called out to know who it was. One fell, I think. your bedroom door must have been ajar. I heard it slam before the man fell down. I do not think he was hurt. He said nothing and did not cry out, and I heard people running away. I searched, to make sure that he was not injured and lying on the ground. There was nobody. I came to your room as quickly as I could, but I heard you moving, and I knew that you had come to no harm. Then you switched on your torch, and, afterwards, the light.'

'Well, well, well!' said Mrs Bradley.

'Do you think you should find out whether you have been robbed?' the nun enquired.

'I have not been robbed,' said Mrs Bradley. 'I doubt whether robbery was the motive,' she added thoughtfully. 'I wonder whether he dropped anything when he fell?'

As soon as she had finished her sherry she went into the garden with her torch and searched the ground below her window. She found what she sought, but not immediately, for it had fallen into a bush. It was a knife of the kind that seamen use.

'Very nice,' she said, when, indoors, she had examined it. 'Quiet and effective. Now I wonder to whom I owe these kind attentions?'

She rang up Pirberry in the morning. Later in the day one of the boys came out early from lessons and asked to speak to her.

'I have Sister's permission,' said he.

'Say on, child,' said Mrs Bradley, giving him her attention.

'Sister Mary Sebastian sent me into the village this morning for some pencils. I couldn't get any, but two men stopped me and asked me where I lived. I told them, and they asked me to look for a knife in the garden. They said they would give me five shillings if I found it and gave it to them without letting anyone know.'

'And did you find it?' Mrs Bradley enquired, looking into his serious eyes. The boy shook his head.

'I thought the money was too much just for finding a knife. I did look for the knife, but I couldn't see it anywhere. I told Sister Mary Dominic about it, and she sent me out of school to tell you.'

'Well, child,' said Mrs Bradley. 'I'll tell you what I want you to do. I want you to look again. It is possible that the knife has sentimental value for those men. One never knows. As soon as lessons are over, search again. Then go into the village, and either tell the men you cannot find the knife, or, if you do find it, you can give it them. What sort of men did they seem?'

'Just ordinary men.'

'Tall? Short?'

'Not to notice. They were just ordinary.'

'I see. All right, then.'

'And can I take the five shillings if I *do* find the knife?'

'I don't see why not,' said Mrs Bradley. She spent a pleasant and instructive time examining the knife for finger-prints, took care that she did not leave her own, and then went up to her bedroom. She surveyed the landscape to make certain that she was not observed, then she dropped the knife out of the open window into the bushes again.

Mr Pirberry was plaintive when she saw him.

'But the fingerprints, ma'am! They might have been invaluable to us!'

'They *will* be invaluable to us,' she replied. 'I have them. You shall develop the photographs yourself.'

'Couldn't you have kept the knife, ma'am? Why did you throw it away?'

'For the sake of the little boy. If he had not been able to find the knife and to tell them exactly where he found it, I don't think he would have lived so very much longer. They would know that he could describe them, and they would guess that I had the knife with their prints – or the prints of one of them –

upon it. As it is, they have no suspicions, I hope, that the knife had ever been found before the boy found it in the bushes.'

Pirberry accepted this view.

'Seems to me, what with the lady nun that chased them off, and this boy who has the decency to think more of his obligations than of five shillings, which must seem the deuce of a lot to an orphan lad,' he said slowly, 'you needn't regret having taken 'em into your house, that's one thing, ma'am.'

'These things are always bread upon the waters,' said Mrs Bradley, grinning.

The Inspector, uncertain whether this was jest or earnest, did not attempt to reply, but asked her whether the boy was able to describe the two men.

'No. They were ordinary,' she replied.

'Like all the best criminals,' said Pirberry gloomily. 'People with horrible scars, or fiery eyes, always turn out to be harmless. Do you think they were Hankin and Brent?'

'I happen to know that they were not Hankin and Brent,' said Mrs Bradley. 'They were dressed in blue jerseys, merchant seamen's caps and pea-jackets, and so bore a superficial likeness to them, but physically there was not the faintest resemblance.'

'And did you know those fellows at all? Had you seen them at the *Cat's Whisker*, for example?'

'No, I am certain I have never seen them before.'

'And yet they tried to knife you?'

'Unless they thought Mr Harben was still at *The Island*, and he was to have been the one attacked.'

'Oh, yes, much more likely,' said Pirberry.

'You know, I doubt that,' said Mrs Bradley. 'I think the man who came with that knife knew perfectly well where David was. No, I'm a nuisance in some way or another, I'm pleased to think.'

'Then you'd better be careful, ma'am. There are plenty of dark alleys in Soho,' said Pirberry sombrely.

# CHAPTER NINETEEN

## *Prodigal*

On a wonderful April morning Harben came back to *The Island*. Sister Mary Dominic saw him first. The time was half-past nine, and Sister Mary Dominic was returning from Mass, which she attended at the Catholic church two and a half miles off in the little town of Helsey, from which the village of Helsey Marsh took its name.

She walked both ways, and Mrs Bradley fed her (with a solicitous tenderness which tickled the nuns, who took it in turns to make the pilgrimage), as soon as she returned to the house.

Harben caught up with her along the towing path, for, although the riverside walk was rather longer than the more direct route along the road, it was, on a fine spring morning, very much more pleasant, and the soft path made easier walking than did the military metal of the road.

Kingcups in fat green bud and shining yellow were showing on every brookside, where the tiny tributaries were lined with the willows which told their course over miles of flat riverside country. Birds skimmed the blue and silver water, or rose to the April sky. The air, with a tender, nostalgic breeze so faint that it did not stir the sedges, was neither cool nor warm, but seemed, like angels' breath, of another sphere. The brambles crept greenish sometimes over the path, the little thorn-trees, fairy-planted, grotesque and goblin-shaped, were in brilliant leaf, and even the red-brown mud of the river bank looked like a clean new bed for the waterside plants.

The grass in the fields was short; there was none of the purple splendour and lush gold-green of the summer. The year was virginal still, and the grass was springing on sleepy ground still sodden from winter bogs. Harben stepped on to it, however, and came up with Sister Mary Dominic before she was aware of his approach. He had taken to calling her Mary, which shocked and amused her; not that she was shocked at his using a Christian name, nor amused because it was part of her name in religion but not the name by which she had been known in the world before she had joined the Dominicans. She was shocked because his use of the name projected the kind of relationship she had foresworn for ever; she was amused because he seemed to derive satisfaction from what he realized must be her reactions to his thoughts.

'Good morning, Mary,' he said; and fell into step beside her.

'Good morning, David,' she answered, giving him a smile which had all of the morning in it. Then she said, but not with surprise, 'You've come back?'

'Did you think I wouldn't?'

'We feared you had run into danger. We heard you had been to the house – the house where such dreadful things happen.'

'They happened to me,' he said. 'I was knocked on the head. I did not come to myself until I was far out to sea in an open boat with no food and scarcely any water.'

He told her all his adventures. They lasted until *The Island* and its dozen neat neighbours came in view. He was silent then, until they were within thirty yards of the lane by which they could gain admission to the house. Then he said:

'And how have you all been getting on?'

'The boys are all well,' she answered. 'Sister Mary Sebastian has prayed for you. Mrs Lestrange Bradley has been all over Soho looking for you – '

'And you?' he interrupted. 'How have *you* been getting on, Mary?'

'Just as usual,' she answered. He glanced quizzically at her.

'You'll have to go to Confession after that. That's a black lie,' he said.

She said, 'I have missed you, and I have prayed for you, of course.'

'A half-truth, but I'll let you off the rest. Well, here we are, and now to confront the old lady.

\* \* \*

'I don't see how you deduced that conversation, ma'am,' said Pirberry, very respectfully.

'Do you not?' said Mrs Bradley. 'It may not be word for word, but as an intelligent reconstruction it isn't far wrong. Unfortunately, as you know, Mr Harben's description of his travels, as confided to Sister Mary Dominic and myself – and I compared notes carefully with her before I gave you the account which you have had – was very little help in solving the mystery of his own disappearance, and the mystery of the old man's death and the strange removal of the body.'

'I can see now why you didn't place too much faith in it, ma'am. Although where they could have got to, all the same, him and the green-eyed young lady . . .'

'His story has not been disproved, as I said before,' said Mrs Bradley.

'Not all of it, ma'am,' agreed Pirberry.

Harben, on his return, seemed to have lost his fear of the lurking men with the boat-hook, and went for a swim every morning just before breakfast. He was rather edgy and nervy, partly because his book struck a snag, as he called it, and partly because he was fretting, for, to his great disappointment, the Admiralty, to whom he had applied again upon his return, had not, so far, written to him again.

He got out the tub, brought her along to the boat-house of *The Island*, and overhauled her completely. Then he went down-river to have another look at the house. He went ashore in the dinghy, drew it up on the wet and shining gravel, and walked across the shingle and up the stone steps. He strolled past the house once or twice, glancing up at it as he passed, but it seemed to be deserted, and he could not make up his mind to knock at the door.

The last time he passed it he walked as far as the bridge. There were plenty of people about, for the weather was fine and warm, and he reflected upon the difference between that fine warm day with its people, and the moonlight night of almost a year ago when the old man had died in the house, and Leda had come down to the tub.

On his return, he met the foreman of the boat-builder's yard, a grizzled man, brown-faced, stiff-bearded, with sloping, strong shoulders and hands like the wood with which he built his boats.

He greeted Harben, expressed pleasure at seeing him again, and drew out a piece of paper.

'I don't know whether you've still got a boat in commission, Mr Harben?'

Harben pointed her out.

'Oh ah. That's her,' said the man. 'Well, I'll have to give you the tip, sir, and it's serious. Every boat that'll keep out water will soon be required, and urgent.'

'What's it all about?' asked Harben. The old man lowered his voice.

'We haven't been let know that, sir. Only, we've had our orders. Navigators, deck-hands, amateur yachtsmen, tug-owners, pleasure-boats – I mean the river steamers, sir, and them that goes round by Margate from Tower Pier – our orders is to warn the whole lot of you you'd better stand by to help the soldiers.'

'Not a German invasion?' asked Harben. The foreman shook his head.

''Taint to be known,' said he, 'but there's doings along the river and over to France. As you've still got a boat, sir, you'll need to be ready to use it. Great doings there is, for them Germans has marched into Belgium and 'Olland, and got the other foreigners on the run. Mr Olney told me. Never hadn't ought to, but 'e did. Take my tip, sir. You get your tank filled up, and a bit of tommy aboard. Nothing won't come amiss. And a life-saving jacket or two, and some brandy and rum. There's the whole bloomin' Expeditionary Force out there.'

Harben laughed.

'Belgium and Holland invaded!' he said. 'Oh, rubbish Tom! Where did you get that tale from?'

But it was all in the morning papers. Mrs Bradley had had the same story from Pirberry, earlier in the day.

'There might be a job for Mr Harben,' Pirberry had informed her. 'You say, ma'am, he's overhauled his boat.'

'He's on the river today. I don't know where he has gone, but I'll hazard a guess.'

'Chasing that girl at the house by the river,' said Pirberry. 'Some young gentlemen are fools. Anyway,' he continued, 'if he likes to run down to the estuary within the next three days, no doubt he'll get marching orders. Then, if he comes back, no doubt I can question him, ma'am.'

'Good heavens!' said Mrs Bradley. 'I knew things have gone very badly, but are they as bad as all that – that he might not return?'

'They're almost as bad as they can be,' Pirberry answered. 'The Belgians are falling back and the French are finished. All the roads to the coast are blocked with refugees, and we've got to get the soldiers away, ma'am, by some of the channel ports, and nothing short of a miracle's going to do it.'

Harben left the tub at her moorings and returned to *The Island* by train. Next day he was back at the moorings and, with expert help, took down and overhauled, for the second time in a month, his powerful engine. Then he ran the tub back to *The Island* to break the news to his friends that he was to leave them again.

When the orphan boys, who had welcomed him back with that disinterested enthusiasm that only children can show, learned that he was leaving again very soon, they were inconsolable.

'But what about our seamanship tests, sir? You said you'd get us to pass them!'

'Won't you show me that star-knot, sir? I've got a bit of rope. *She* gave it me.'

This formidable title indicated their hostess. Sister Mary Dominic gently, Harben wrathfully, corrected it whenever they heard it. Harben corrected it now.

'*She?* Who's *She?*'

'Mrs Lestrange Bradley, sir.'

'Why the dickens don't you say so, then?'

'Very sorry, sir. But where are you going to?'

The last afternoon was brilliant. It was nearly the end of May. Harben was to set out on the following morning. The sun was high, and Harben was sprawled near Sister Mary Dominic's chair in the pleasant, lush, riverside garden, resting on his

elbows, chewing grass and gazing across the river. He heard her
rustling the pages of her book. He looked round at her, saw the
title of the book, and sat up.

'Where did you get that?' he asked.

'Mrs Bradley lent it me. I asked for it.'

'But why on earth?'

'I think I may have misjudged you. I want to know more
about you than I do.'

Harben laughed, but he knew that she was serious. But what
more was there to know? She had known a good deal about him
when she and Sister Sebastian had first come aboard the tub,
and by this time she knew as much about him as he knew about
himself. She knew that he was impulsive and could be gentle.
She knew (although he would not have admitted this himself)
that he was rashly chivalrous and kind. She knew that he wrote,
but neither he nor she knew, or could ever know, what was the
basis of the unavoidable compulsion under which he wrote; a
compulsion which nagged at him even when he was not writing.
She knew – to descend to more mundane but not less important
matters – that he had enough money to live on, even without his
writing. She knew that his mother had died when he was five,
and that his father had left him money. She knew how much
money it was, and thought it very little, for she came of a
wealthy family.

She knew that he was communicative, not secret; that he was,
on the whole, an idler, for he confessed that he never worked
regularly, even at his writing, but only by fits and starts. She
knew that he detested beginning a book and was depressed when
it was finished. She knew that, almost as soon as he had finished
one book, he felt compelled to begin another.

She knew that he had friends; that, often, he did not see them
nor write to them from one year's end to the next.

Having answered him, she bent her head over the pages, and
read, with intense concentration, the words which he had
written.

Harben left gazing at the river and watched her as she read,
and tried to imagine her in the life she had led before the war.

He tried to imagine her, first of all, at morning. He could
fancy how she would put on her white serge gown and above it

her scapula. The gown would reach almost to the floor of her cell, but would clear it sufficiently to show (although not her white stockings) the buckles of her broad black shoes. The gown had wide sleeves reaching to the wrists, and underneath those sleeves she would have fastened others, detachable and close-fitting, which were made to button neatly on to the short sleeves of her flannel petticoat. He knew this because Sister Sebastian had told him so when they were discussing the Dominican habit.

The scapula was an over-garment consisting merely of a front and a back panel of serge. Beneath it, so that the beads could be seen in graceful loops at her left side, was a fifteen-decade rosary.

Above the scapula she would put on the white linen gimp which covered her shoulders and the upper part of her breast, and above it, around her head, she would fasten a stiff white linen binder and surmount it with her long black veil.

Yes; he knew all about the Dominican habit from Sister Sebastian, for if there was one thing above all others which could give Sister Sebastian an almost sinful feeling of pride, it was this white serge uniform, of which, Sister Sebastian had informed him, every fold and fall and fastening had to be as exact and correct as that of a soldier on parade. The belt of stout leather from which the rosary hung was braced like a soldier's belt, and the long black cloak was analogous to a military cape, for Dominicans, like their founder, had the soldierly mind, he had learned.

The Order was an active one. Doctors, fully qualified nurses, trained teachers, domestic science experts, social workers, super-intendents of hostels, were to be found among its members. Some Houses specialized in one kind of work and some in another, but the sisters were never allowed to forget that their founder had lived and worked in the world, and not in the cloister; had been a preacher and a missionary, not a mystic, a contemplative or a visionary.

Harben, nodding acceptance of these facts, had also learned from Sister Sebastian that Sister Mary Dominic came of one of the oldest Catholic families in England, and could have shown (had she been at home) the priest's hole where protagonists of the martyr Edmund Campion had lain hidden, and the blackened east wall where a company of Levellers had set fire to the family mansion at the time of the Civil War.

Now another and a deadlier war was afoot. Other Catholic priests in Occupied Europe had suffered and were to suffer a fate as bloody as Campion's; towns, not separate houses, were to be burned and devastated until civilization itself was fighting to live. Whole countrysides were to be blasted by high explosive, proud cities and then whole countries were to fall and yield and be enslaved. Satan was out of hell, and his legions of furies and devils were loosed on a world grown slack and careless, on people absorbed in little lovings and hatreds, coarse pleasures and dirty little sins. So Sister Mary Sebastian had told Harben, interspersing her words with comforting pictures of Heaven.

Still regarding the peach-down cheek, the delicate mouth and the sweep of black lashes over eyes that were bent on the book, he continued his mental exercises, imagining Sister Mary Dominic in the life described by the older, more genial nun. At five minutes to seven, the Sisters went to their chapel. There they made meditation until seven-thirty, when the Little Hours of Prime, Terce, Sext and None were recited by the choir sisters, whilst the lay sisters went to work. Then followed Mass, attended by all whose duties allowed them to come. At a quarter to nine Mass ended and breakfast was served. He could see the prim lines, the orderly heads, the clean, fresh, morning faces of the nuns, and, among them, the lovely head of Sister Mary Dominic. He sighed, and she looked up immediately, as though, underneath her outward and visible concentration, she was as much aware of him as he of her.

'Well?' he said. 'And what do you make of the masterpiece?'

'Nothing very much,' she answered. She closed the book, but kept a finger between the pages. 'I think' – she looked earnestly at him – 'you will not be offended – ?'

'Of course not. You'd never offend me, no matter what you said.'

'Well, I still think you have some very silly ideas.'

They both laughed. Then he said soberly:

'Silly? You don't say wicked?'

'No. I don't say wicked. I think you were young for your age when you wrote this book.'

'Yes,' he said, sober still, and thinking suddenly of Leda. 'Yes, I was young for my age.'

'Then I have learnt something from your book,' she said; and this time she closed it and stood up.

'Don't go,' said Harben. 'It's the loveliest thing in life to sit with you in a garden. You're so beautifully restful and quiet. You're like the river – restful and quiet – and eternal.'

'I must go,' she said, taking no more notice of the words than she would take, presently, of falling autumn leaves. 'We live, you know, by the sun.'

'By the clock,' he said, a little bitterly. 'I wonder you don't get tired of it all. Do you – ever?'

'No,' she said, giving the question her complete consideration. 'Rhythm is what God has ordered. The sun rises and sets at its appointed time, and the grass grows and flowers blossom and fade. So with us. We are working and praying, feasting and fasting, grieving, rejoicing, living every year the life of Our Blessed Lord. Only Satan grows tired of the rhythm of earth and heaven.'

She returned the book the next day. Mrs Bradley thanked her, and asked politely whether she had enjoyed it.

'It is so sinful,' said Sister Mary Dominic, sadly. 'And he – he is not sinful at all, except as we all are, according to our mortal nature. I have brothers. I know what makes a good man. And he is good. Why does he write like that?'

'Yes, he is good,' agreed her hostess, returning the book to a shelf, and not attempting to answer the question.

'You do not talk to me,' said Sister Mary Dominic. 'Why is that?'

'Because you would find my thoughts and opinions either objectionable or incomprehensible,' replied Mrs Bradley concisely. 'You and I, child, must be content to run along parallel lines. They *are* parallel lines, you know.'

'Yes,' said the nun, with a sudden, most wonderful smile. 'Yes, may God bless you. I know.'

# BOOK SIX

## Dunkirk

*

Last came, and last did go
The pilot of the Galilean lake.

John Milton

---

### CHAPTER TWENTY

## *Beaches*

Harben backed gently away from *The Island's* riverside wall, and then, reversing the engine, began to slide rapidly downstream.

The weather was calm and fine, the cruise down-river uneventful. It occurred to him that he might be going to his death, and so he allowed himself to stop off by the house where Leda had lived, and moor there for the night.

He went ashore just after dark, Mrs Bradley's revolver in his right hand, an electric torch in his left, mounted the steps of the house and knocked at the door. No one replied to his knocking. He tried again. But not a glimmer of light nor the stifled sound of a movement gave him any reward. He went slowly back to the tub and slept on board.

He was casting off at daybreak when he saw a white-robed Dominican coming along the concrete path. She was so much like Sister Mary Dominic in the distance that he did not start up his engine, but watched her coming along, incongruous in that place of his other life. It *was* Sister Mary Dominic. He took her aboard without a word.

She offered no explanation; he asked no questions. He smiled at her as she took her seat in the well.

At Greenwich the tub was stopped by river police, and Harben was asked his business and destination.

'I heard they wanted small craft to cross to France,' he said. His papers were examined, the officer smiled, wished him good luck, told him to look out for floating mines off the Estuary, and on went the tub. At Woolwich he was stopped once more, but after that he got down as far as Tilbury, and there had instructions to go with all possible speed to Dover Harbour, or, if the harbour were full, to lie off in the Downs. As this coincided with earlier orders, he merely engaged his engine and sped away.

His little craft bucketed badly in the tidal streams of the Estuary. It was five hours after high water at Dover, so he came out on the ebb past the lightship *Tongue*, then headed south for the *North Goodwin*, thankful that, with his shallow draught, he need make no allowance for sand.

Past North Foreland and Ramsgate they ran, and down past Deal and Walmer, inclined with the coast at Hope Point and Saint Margaret's Bay, and then bent south-west at South Foreland and sighted the long breakwater which marked, in time of peace, the ferry to Calais.

Other breakwaters enclosed the harbour, which already was crowded with craft. The tub, which, in spite of her clumsy, ungainly appearance, was well engined and could develop a speed of eighteen miles an hour, arrived at the harbour in the early evening, and wriggled in close to the pier. Harben went ashore for instructions, was issued with duplicate charts of the channels leading into the harbour of Dunkirk, and was able to give an assurance that his compass was properly adjusted and that he was provisioned. He asked for fuel, and got it, was warned of mines and the possibility of attack, learned that he would have to be prepared to embark men from open beaches, and promised that when he was loaded he would re-embark his passengers on the larger craft which would be lying off-shore, and go back, if he could, for another load.

'We can't tell you in detail what you have to expect,' said the officer who was directing him. 'The mess out there is bound to be pretty frightful, and you may find you'll have to rely entirely on your own mother wit.'

They had forty miles to cover to reach Dunkirk. They crossed, on strangely smooth water, in two and a half hours. It was then growing dark. The town, which they had seen from two or three miles out because of the smoke that hung over it, was lighted by spurts of flame. The noise of guns and of bombing was thunderous and almost monotonous. A bomber came over them twice, and sprayed the sea. Showers of vicious machine-gun bullets spattered the water like rain. The plane flew off to attack a larger target. Harben look at Sister Mary Dominic, raised his eyebrows and received her answering smile.

'I'm going in now,' he said. They could see the beaches; the sand-dunes uneven and greyish; the black forms of men, and the hulls of the warships standing off from the harbour.

Small boats were already picking up soldiers from smashed pier and broken quays, from the beaches and out of the sea. Some of the men had waded towards the boats. Harben could see long lines of them, orderly and quiet, in the water.

He picked out a likely stretch of the shore and cut out his engine. An officer was marshalling men. There seemed to be no disorder, although the noise of the guns and the planes was now unceasing.

Harben loaded up and backed out cautiously, then turned and made for a destroyer. He made ten trips before dark.

Bombs made the sea like a storm. Twice he thought that the tub would lift her engine out of its bed, but everything settled again. The night came on, but the work did not diminish. The sea had been black with craft, many of which were now invisible, but a lurid light from the burning town lit up large areas of water. Planes flew over the beaches and bombs dropped every few minutes, but most of the men were in sandholes, and the target, after dark, was unsatisfactory, although the enemy sent up flares, and the bombs began falling again on the whitened landscape.

All night the work went on. As they lay off after taking on or disembarking troops, Harben and Sister Mary Dominic could hear the splash of oars and the low-toned voices of sailors. It was one of the most eerie experiences of Harben's life – this hearing of quiet, civilized, decent voices and with them the sounds of summer, the plash and the creaking of oars, and after them the crashing guns, and the screaming and whining of the bombs, and then the silence again.

'It is like Christ walking on the water,' said Sister Mary Dominic in his ear. 'After all the tumult, so calm, so good.'

The voices faded; the sound of the oars passed into the sound of the light waves washing on the shore. There was no drag of shingle to give a harsh reality to the sea. It was halcyon sea, a children's sea, the more so in contrast with all the horror of the day.

By dawn it was time to get away. Harben needed more petrol, and Sister Mary Dominic needed more medical supplies. They returned to the beach once more and brought off ten men and their officer. The sky began to grow grey.

'Come along, sir,' said Harben. The officer glanced back uncertainly, but all his party was aboard, and so he followed. The tub backed off again, turned, and tore off towards a destroyer. Her commander told them that he had orders to be off, as the harbour would be hell as soon as the sun was up.

'Right,' said Harben; and made for the beach once more. An officer, limping, asked him whether he could take any wounded aboard.

'Only if they can sit up,' was Harben's reply.

'It's only one fellow; a lieutenant. We'll bring him,' said the officer. A plane flew over directly he had left them, coughed out bullets on to the loose, coarse sand, and dropped a couple of bombs in the shallow sea. The tub gave a hiccough and rocked, but she was not grounded, and, having registered a protest by breaking most of the crockery which had not, so far, been broken, she settled down again.

A sergeant embarked a dozen men, and then they all waited. At last the officer reappeared with three more, one of whom the others were carrying on a four-handed seat. They all made heavy going over the sand, but gained the edge at last. It was difficult to get the wounded lieutenant into the boat. Harben waded ashore and lent a hand

They got back to Dover for breakfast – a rather late breakfast. They rested, refuelled, reprovisioned, and set out again at seven o'clock in the evening by the route which they had used both going out and returning. It was the shortest route of the three which were recommended – just thirty-nine sea miles – and took them almost to Calais before the tub turned at an angle of an hundred and thirty degrees to slant north-east along the sandy coast between the Mardick and Snouw Banks, where it converged upon the longer, fifty-five-mile route from the North Goodwin Lightship. This track crossed the Outer Ruytingen and then slanted south past La Dyck. Off Snouw Bank and Brack Bank were the Dunkirk Roads.

Their first trip had been on a Sunday. The troopships had set out during the afternoon. On this next day, Monday, the bombing from German aeroplanes was worse. British fighters were outnumbered fifty to one as they strove to protect the crowded sea and the equally crowded port and its blackened beaches. Harben worked dry-mouthed and with pricking skin, but Sister Mary Dominic seemed without fear. The seas were heavier than on the previous day. Some naval ratings told Harben that the Atlantic weather was stormy. Earlier he had been told that Calais had fallen. The news of the weather seemed a good deal more serious to him.

Fortunately, the worst of the weather passed northwards, but there came an ugly swell which swamped the small boats on the beaches, and made it extremely difficult to get men off from the shore. Harben rigged up a tow line, and took off ships' boats full of soldiers, but he heard that up at the docks and in the harbour matters were going badly. He himself made less than half the number of trips he had made on the previous night, and the tub did everything but founder, and rolled and complained as she hogged to the beaches and back.

They were off at dawn again, whilst the aeroplanes moaned overhead and flares went up, and the burning town smouldered red, and the men on the beaches coughed out the acrid smoke. The German guns kept up an incessant shelling, and streams of tracer bullets picked out the British planes. The bombing was not quite so bad now, for appalling clouds of smoke from the burning town hid everything else from view.

The threatened stormy weather had passed over, but next day they saw a ship sunk by collision in the Dunkirk Roads, and had to take off survivors. They transported these to a vessel hove-to nearby, and then got on with the beachwork. It was automatic now, and Harben, with next day's dawn, was preparing to get back to Dover when a bomb fell very close and the repercussion lifted the engine of the tub and smashed the compass.

Harben had been putting in to the beach to take off his last load. Except for himself and the nun, the tub was empty. He scrambled up from where he had flung himself across her, and switched off the useless and possibly dangerous engine. He asked her whether she was hurt, and held her against him, as people hold children who have suffered a bad fall or shock.

'No,' she answered; but her face was very white and she breathed fast and short, and held his sleeve tightly, unconscious that she did so.

'You get below,' said Harben. 'I'll come as soon as I can. Lie down on one of the bunks.'

'No, I shall manage,' she said.

'You'll do as you're told,' said he, and kissed her.

'Yes,' she said, with sudden, meek, and, to him, surprising obedience. He did not dare to leave the wheel to go and look after her. It was not yet light, and suddenly, over the side, a voice called:

'Boat, ahoy!'

'Where are you?' cried Harben, leaning over.

'Here!'

'I'm not under control. You'll have to find me,' called Harben. He took out an electric torch and shone it on the water. Almost immediately there was the drone of a plane overhead.

'Cut it out, mate! The B's have spotted you!' called the voice.

'Come on, then,' said Harben. The drone of the plane grew fainter. He shone the torch again, and a hand came up from the sea and clutched the gunwale. It was difficult to get the man aboard. It was a sailor.

'Any more of you!' asked Harben.

'Should be, mate. They caught us a proper lick. Cut away half the bows, I shouldn't wonder.'

'All right. I'll hang about, as long as I don't drift too far in. Can't see to do a decent job, anyway, until it gets light.'

He kept his eyes on the water, and strained his ears. No more men approached him, but when it grew lighter he saw them, six or seven, although it was hard to tell in that faint light, which were heads and which the wreckage with which the sea was strewn. The tub had drifted dangerously near the shore. Harben lowered his fisherman's anchor, and then, with the help of the sailor, set the auxiliary sails he always carried.

'How long you been on this game, sir?' asked the sailor, looking at Harben's face and stubble of beard.

'All the time since the beginning,' Harben answered. 'But I'm dished this time, I'm afraid. If I run this tub on to the beach I'll never get her off this side of Christmas, and we're shockingly near shoal water. Take the wheel, while I see to the damage.'

The engine had been lifted out of its bed, and, with it, the forward planking of the cockpit. Sister Mary Dominic got up.

'The men must come in and rest,' she said. 'I am better.'

'No wounded this time,' said Harben; but she would not stay in the cabin.

There was a heavy surf on the beach that morning, and although the long length of anchor chain which Harben had thought best to let out on a sandy bottom had held the tub well whilst the work of setting the sails was going forward, unfortunately the wind continued to blow towards the shore. Harben raised anchor, and tacked as well as he could, but the tub's ungainly superstructure acted as a trap for the wind, and she was gradually driven back towards the beach. A ship's boat, coming alongside, asked if he were in trouble, and offered to come back, as soon as it had unloaded, to take off his people. But the tide was on the turn, and they drifted off-shore again, and gained the thick of the smoke at the harbour entrance.

Harben manoeuvred his craft half-way to Dover. Then a naval cutter gave him a tow.

* * *

'And was the Sister hurt badly, ma'am?' asked Pirberry.

'She was bruised all over, as I found when he got her home,' said Mrs Bradley. 'No bones were broken. It took the tow fifteen hours to get back to Dover. It must have been a terrible time. Provisions and water were short, but everyone on board seemed content, and nobody grumbled. The sailors took it in turns to sleep in the cabin.

'And why, ma'am, have you told me this tale?' asked Pirberry.

'Because,' said Mrs Bradley, 'I wanted to paint the picture of a man who is not a poisoner. You now know as much about the affair as I do myself, and from this point we set our wits to work to discover who caused the old man's death – or, rather, to prove our suspicions.'

'I quite see you don't think Mr Harben's weapon would be poison, however much he might want a man out of the way. And you mean that Mr Harben wasn't all that dead set on the green-eyed young lady, after all, or he wouldn't have fallen quite so hard for the nun. And you mean the old fellow might easily have had it coming to him from the Spaniards, especially if they are the young lady's brothers. There's plenty in what you suggest, ma'am, but I think Mr Harben's got a lot of explaining to do.'

# BOOK SEVEN

# This Side of Heaven

*

And when all bodies meet
In Lethe to be drowned,
Then only numbers sweet
With endless life are crowned.

Herrick

---

## CHAPTER TWENTY-ONE

# *Spaniards*

This explaining Harben was soon called upon to do. The Spanish captain and The Louse having come out of hospital, Pirberry found no difficulty in rounding them up, and he brought in with them the other members of their crew, the sinister mate Don Juan, a deck-hand called Estéban and the ship's cook, a fat and genial-looking fellow known as Jorge.

The Spaniards had been vouched for by their Consulate, and it was in the full odour of sanctity, as Mrs Bradley put it, that they made their appearance in Pirberry's office.

'Ah, Mr Harben!' said the Spanish captain. 'How is your honour? We meet at a good time. You must tell your policemen, please, not to put us in prison, as we are under the protection of our Embassy, are distressed seamen, and are known at the Consulate as good and reasonable men.'

'That's all right,' said Harben.

'Yes,' said the captain in Spanish, 'but look here! What do they want us for?'

'They want to know why you are here,' replied Harben. The captain shrugged, and Don Juan responded angrily:

'We have been attacked. That is why we are here.'

'U-boats?' asked Pirberry, through the interpreter.

'No, no. Surface raiders.'

'They say,' said the interpreter, 'that their ship has been attacked by surface raiders.'

'Where?' demanded Pirberry.

'In Spanish waters. Off Corŭna.'

'Why are they in England? Shouldn't they have put in to Spain?'

'They were rescued by a British ship, they say. It put in at a South Coast port.'

'We shall have to get that story verified,' said Pirberry. 'Of course, they're neutrals, and all that, but it sounds a bit fishy to me. Ask them what a British ship was doing in Spanish waters.'

The interpreter did so, and replied:

'They say the British ship was bringing back people from Lisbon. Refugees from France, the Riviera and Switzerland.'

'That sounds a bit more likely. All right. When we've done with them over this business, I suppose we can get them back to Gibraltar somehow, and they'll have to make their own way home from there, if the Gib. authorities will let them.'

The Spaniards were then closely questioned about the attacks made on them in Soho. They professed complete ignorance of the reason for the attacks, and protested that they had been made on Mr Harben. Harben concurred in this view, but declared that he could offer no explanation.

'You were subject to other attacks, sir, I believe, at the very beginning of the war,' said Pirberry, when the Spaniards, after an exchange of compliments between themselves and the police, had been allowed to return to their lodgings. Harben glanced reproachfully at Mrs Bradley. 'And to what do you attribute these favours, sir?' continued Pirberry, with an irony which startled his hearers.

'Attribute . . . I haven't the slightest idea why I should be set upon.'

'Are you certain of that, sir?'

'Of course I am. I can't help it if there are criminal lunatics about.'

'I see, sir. Well, that's that, then.' And Pirberry nodded to the policeman near the door to show him out. When he was gone, Pirberry turned to Mrs Bradley.

'Something very fishy there, ma'am, I don't care what you say.'

'Oh, I don't know,' said Mrs Bradley. 'One must be tolerant and reasonably imaginative, don't you think? After all . . .'

'After all, he may still think he's shielding the young lady. Yes, I allow for that, ma'am. He may have come to some agreement with these Spaniards.'

When she had left New Scotland Yard, Mrs Bradley telephoned Harben, who had found refuge at the flat of a friend in Soho Square.

'The police are very much interested in your Spanish friends,' she said. 'They are not quite clear yet how they come to be in England, and they are chary of accepting their story. Can they be telling the truth?'

'I don't know,' answered Harben. 'But I'll tell you what I can do. I'll take them out for a pub-crawl, and see what I can get out of them, if you like.'

'I really cannot advise it,' she replied. She heard the full story later. The Spaniards, despite all war-time restrictions and the black-out, spent a most festive evening, followed, everywhere they went, by the police. This precautionary measure was the result of collusion between Pirberry and Mrs Bradley, although their motives were quite dissimiliar.

When the party could obtain no more drinks, it occurred to Harben (by this time considerably fuddled) to take his party to sleep at the house by the river. He led them down the steps of the Piccadilly Tube, bought tickets, took the owlish El Piojo by the arm, and led him to the escalator. El Piojo, who was country bred, drew back, but the others, their grave Spanish faces never changing, thrust him on, and, a stout gentleman in a bowler hat and carrying a gasmask acting as buffer, he arrived safely at the bottom. Having discovered that the escalator did him no harm, he leapt on to the second one with a shout of '*La montana! La montana!*' Then he proceeded to tear headlong down, taking off his cap to the patient English who he inconvenienced as he burst excitedly past them.

'He has negro blood,' said the Spanish captain, negligently, to Harben. 'And he is, of course, a madman.'

Harben retained, even in his cups, an English sense of responsibility. He dashed after El Piojo, and discovered him at the bottom of the escalator weeping, and pointing to the passage through which they had to pass to get to the trains.

'It is hell,' said he, 'is it not? Why have you brought me here, my friend?'

'It is not hell. It is the train,' said Harben, taking his arm and leading him into the tunnel. 'But if you want to see hell, you shall. I will take you to it tonight.'

They got El Piojo on to the train, which, at that time of night, was almost empty, and he fell asleep immediately he sat down. Don Juan, who was seated next to him, leaned across and touched Harben's knee.

'I trust you entirely,' said he, 'but where do you take us?'

'To the house by the river,' said Harben.

'And we shall sleep there?'

'Certainly.'

'I thank you, sir. I am satisfied that you are a man of honour,' said the mate.

'I thank you, too,' replied Harben, closing his eyes. 'You are, without doubt, the most honest man in Seville.'

'I have never been in Seville, sir.'

'I beg your pardon, sir. I should have said . . .?'

'You should have said Andalusia, sir. It is wider,' said Don Juan, demonstrating.

'Many thanks for your valuable correction, sir.'

They all slept. A kindly stranger turned them out at Hammersmith, the station at which they had to change.

Harben, dry-mouthed and feeling slightly sick, began to wonder, as they waited in the dark for a District train, whether his idea had really been such a good one after all. However, he could scarcely desert the Spaniards now. They crowded on to a train, got out at Chiswick Park, and walked the rest of the way.

It was a good long walk, and the blackness was so intense that

Harben, who was gradually regaining his senses, also began to wonder whether they would not be just as likely to tumble into the river as to gain the house which they sought. But it was too late to think of that. However, they were fortunate enough to fall in with a man who had a torch, and, linking arms across the narrow street which led to the river, they followed the gleam until their guide entered a house and left them in the pitch-black night.

'This way,' said Harben. With difficulty they negotiated the narrow turning and passed between the three white posts which marked the junction of the road with the concrete path along which they would have to go to get to the house.

Harben was afraid that they might walk past it in the blackness. There was nothing to show which house it was, unless he could find the pillared portico. He tried to remember, as they felt their way along – he and El Piojo in the lead, the captain and Don Juan close behind them, and Estéban and Jorge bringing up the rear – exactly where the house was situated.

The Spaniards walked steadily, said nothing, and appeared to be able to see, like cats, in the dark, for they made no complaints and never trod on the heels of those in front. Even El Piojo was quiet, and seemed to be in full possession of his faculties.

The blackness, as is its wont, grew appreciably less black as they proceeded, and Harben could fancy at last that he could see a dull gleam from the river. He found the house by coming up suddenly in front of one of the pillars. He stopped short, and the Spaniards following him cannoned into him.

They were gravely and sincerely apologetic.

'Here we are,' he said, in English; and then, in Spanish, 'Take care. There are nine steps.'

They all counted them as they stumbled and groped their way upwards. When he had gained the top of the flight, Harben pushed open the letter-box and peered in. A gleam of light came from under one of the doors. He could see the thin streak across the hall.

He took up the knocker and banged loudly.

'I don't know whether it's my wife or the burglars,' he remarked. Suddenly it became evident that he and the Spaniards were not the only persons on the steps. An English official voice demanded sturdily:

'Now what's all this, gentlemen? You don't live in this house.' The next moment, just before Pirberry's bloodhounds joined them, a policeman's lamp was being flashed in their faces.

'That's all right, officer,' said Harben. Before he could say any more, the shadows who had tracked him and his party from pub to pub in Soho and now by train from Piccadilly and on to the house, began to manifest themselves to the constable.

'And the gentlemen can go into the house if they care to. Those are our orders,' said the shadows.

'Very good,' said the local constable. 'Then good night, all.' He switched off his lamp and felt his way down the steps. They could hear him walking away along the concrete path.

'And now, sir,' said the leader of the shadows, 'we must come in with you if you're going into this house.'

'The more the merrier,' said Harben. There had been no reply to his knocking. He knocked again. This time there was the sound of footsteps coming towards the front door. It was opened. A torch picked out the buttons on his coat, and then travelled up to his face.

'Ah,' said Mrs Bradley. 'I expected you. Pray come in.'

It had been, on the whole, a strange evening. To Harben at this point it became fantastic. All his visits to this house had had a dream-quality unlike anything else he had experienced, and this visit seemed as extraordinary as any of the others. He could not have explained why, but Mrs Bradley was quite the last person by whom he had expected to be confronted.

A fire was burning in the grate. The heavy, thick curtains were drawn closely across the windows, and Harben and the sinister old lady sat opposite one another across the hearth. Of the Spaniards, the captain, Don Juan and Estéban occupied in close contact with one another, an old-fashioned, high-backed couch, whilst El Piojo, lying on the floor at their feet, soon succumbed to slumber, and pillowed his head on Estéban's square-toed boots. Jorge took a chair near the door.

Conversation was carried on chiefly by Mrs Bradley. She would not speak Spanish, and the captain's laboured, oddly inflected English could neither grapple with her questions nor enable him to frame any very satisfactory replies.

At last Mrs Bradley rose. The Spaniards, except for El Piojo, rose politely. He, awakened by the sudden movement of Estéban's boots beneath his head, snorted, sat up, gazed round, sighed deeply, like a dog, and then lay down again.

'Good night, gentlemen,' said Mrs Bradley. 'There are beds for all when you wish for them. Mr Harben will conduct you to your rooms.'

Harben said to the others, in Spanish:

'At your service, gentlemen. This makes a complication. Please follow me. I must see what beds we have.'

The captain and Don Juan took the room in which the old man's body had lain; Jorge had the attic bedroom above in which the old man died. Estéban, who seemed to think that someone should have charge of El Piojo, accepted the attic next to that occupied by Jorge, because it contained two beds. He woke the half-breed and shepherded him upstairs.

Harben went back to the room in which all had sat, for he felt sure that Mrs Bradley would want to communicate with him. He waited for half an hour, but she made no sign. Then he turned sharply, for he heard the creak of the door. It was not Mrs Bradley, but Leda. She came in, put her fingers against the back of his head, stroked the short harsh hairs on his nape, bent her head until her mouth was against his neck, kissed the top of his ear, and sat on the arm of his chair.

'Aren't you coming to bed?' she asked.

Without question he rose and went with her, but, as he stood up, he took out a sailor's knife and carried it in his hand as they went upstairs.

'We must be quiet,' she said.

There seemed nothing to fear, however. She led the way to a room on the garden side of the house. The bed was deep and wide. It was so comfortable, and now that Harben was in it he felt so tired that his only remaining fear was lest he should fall asleep. He had a thousand questions to ask, but they did not exchange another word. They lay close in one another's arms, learning one another again, and bridging the months that had gone with the moment which now seemed their own.

They did not sleep, for at three in the morning the siren, wailing its lost, unearthly, melancholy warning over the ancient houses and older river, brought Leda sitting up in bed, her fingers biting hard into David's arm.

'The cellar!' she said. 'I know it's going to be bad.'

'Are you afraid?' he murmured.

'Not for myself, but I don't want to lose you now.'

She groped her clothes and put them on; found shoes; turned impatiently to him.

'David, be quick! Be quick!'

Harben pulled on his shirt and trousers and a jacket, found socks and shoes, put his hand on the door, and struck a match.

'Blow it out!' she said. 'I know the way, and I don't want to meet the others.'

'But if there's a shelter . . .?'

'Your old lady will show them. She knows where it is.'

They went down the stairs in the dark, and into the garden. There was now a gap in the fence. She pulled him through it. They went down the next-door garden, and, by a ramp, into a shelter.

The shelter was dry and warm. A man was already in it. Harben recognized him as the next-door neighbour who had spoken about the weeds. They greeted one another.

'Yes, it's my shelter,' he said, 'but I don't mind who uses it, of course. The young lady is my guest every night that we have a raid. She often gets here before I do.'

'Yes. I'm afraid of the raids,' said Leda. Harben did not believe she was afraid. He had discovered, he thought, her hiding-place. He was no longer surprised that she had remained undetected. He had fancied she looked very pale. This underground life explained it. He wondered how she had managed to get enough food.

They could hear very little of the raid. Their neighbour went up to the surface to find out how matters were going, and came back to report that the barrage was heavy but that the house and those near it seemed not to be damaged. Whilst he made his third reconnaissance the All Clear signal was given, and they went aloft to a clear and beautiful morning.

'Let's swim,' said Leda.

'Let's go to bed,' said Harben. She was tired, and soon fell asleep. They had drawn back the curtains. The morning light grew stronger. Harben did not sleep. He was wondering how he could keep her now that he had her again. He lolled on his elbow to look at her. Pale, defenceless, vulnerable and childlike she seemed, different from the young girl who had tapped with urgent fingers that night nearly twelve months earlier, yet reminiscent of her in the same way that a face seen dimly in green glass is reminiscent of itself.

Then she had still been her own, and now she was his. Then she had walked with fear, but now the fear was in his own heart, lest he should lose her again.

He woke her at last by taking her into his arms. She woke with a smile, and said at once:

'I've been dreaming about your old lady.'

'Nice or nasty?' said he.

'I don't know. Let's trust her, David. Let's tell her the truth, and – '

'No. Let's swim,' said Harben.

There seemed to be nobody about. The tide was half-way out, and a long spit of ooze and gravel lay between the bottom of the river-bank steps and the stream.

This time they had no tub from which to bathe, so they walked downstream to the cut and took off their clothes behind a hopper which was lying heeled-over on the mud. They tossed their towels into a dinghy drawn up out of reach of high tide on the concrete bottom of the slipway, and waded into the water hand in hand.

Leda was swimming first. She walked in up to her knees, reached forward, threw herself flat, and paddled out with her hands until the water was deep enough for swimming.

Harben, who knew he could not catch her if once she decided to swim fast, swam to amuse himself only. They neither kept together nor made any signal until, as soon as he was tired, he swam up beside a willow bush on the island, sure that she would come up, and so she did.

She did not get out of the water, but lay on her breast by the bank and swayed herself gently forward and backward on her hands.

'Will you stay this time?' asked Harben.

She smiled, looking down at the water, her greenish lashes damp on her wet, cold cheeks. Harben had a sudden recollection of the wonderful, long, black lashes of Sister Mary Dominic, and, startled, blinked it away.

'Shall we tell your old lady?' asked Leda.

'I'm cold,' he said. 'Let's go back.'

They went back to an empty house. Mrs Bradley and the Spaniards were gone. Leda had brought no key. She led him back by way of the shelter belonging to the next-door neighbour. It was built, Harben now discovered, almost at the bottom of this garden. A long passage led to his cellar, which was damp and already contained, with the rising tide, six inches of water. They splashed through this, and gained the cellar of Leda's own house through a large gap which had been picked in the cellar wall. It was new since Harben and Mrs Bradley had found the cellar opening in the pantry.

Up the steps they went; into the kitchen. No one was there. The upstairs rooms, equally, were empty.

'Gone off without having breakfast,' said Harben. 'Queer. I suppose they concluded I'd gone back to town without them. You'd think they'd have seen us in the water.'

Mrs Bradley had gone, by the earliest morning train to her duties in Soho, and had left the house whilst the raid was still on, at just after five o'clock. The Spaniards, who had an aristocratic scorn of bombs and shrapnel, had remained in bed until seven, and then had left, sober and hungry, to get their breakfast in Town. Mistrusting the concrete path, they had taken the first little alley, come on to a road, and the captain's English had been found sufficient to permit him to ask the way to the nearest station.

# CHAPTER TWENTY-TWO

## *Merman*

Pirberry sent for the Spanish captain that afternoon, and asked him again about his wound.

'I know nothing. I say nothing. I dislike the police,' said the captain scornfully.

'But it's a question of murder. And you yourself were pretty badly injured by the fellow, whoever he is,' said Pirberry, through the interpreter.

'With dead men I have no conversation,' said the captain grandly. 'And with the man who attacked me with a knife I have still an account to settle. I shall settle it without the aid of the police.'

'Not in England you won't my bucko,' said Pirberry in English. The interpreter translated this as: 'In England we are all law-abiding citizens.'

The captain smiled politely, and Pirberry, unable to get any more out of him, had to let him go.

'I don't know whether *you* could get any more out of him, ma'am,' he said dejectedly.

'I could tell him the truth, which at present I think he only guesses,' said Mrs Bradley.

'Then there is proof, ma'am, of – ?'

'There's proof strangers came to *The Island*. Why should they have come there? They knew where David was, and they knew he was not with me. They meant to make certain that I was not left alive to tell tales. They knew David and I were friends, and they must have believed he had some special knowledge which could be used against them, and which he might have communicated to me. If he has such knowledge, he is still unaware of the fact. It's interesting. I wonder what it is they thought he knew?'

'Something about the poison, ma'am. It must be.'

'I wonder?' said Mrs Bradley.

'But if they were so determined on getting rid of him, why didn't they kill him when they had the chance? You mentioned that evening outing, ma'am. What did you mean?'

'That David is only afraid of one of them now, not both. He has discovered something since he came back to England – not necessarily about the poison.'

'I suppose they thought they had seen the last of him when they threw him into the open boat and cast him adrift on the sea. It must have given them a terrible shock to run into him again in England,' Pirberry observed. 'How did that happen, do you think, ma'am?'

'I really think Fate stepped in. Their ship was torpedoed or gunned, and they were brought into port here, just as they told us. Their Consulate vouches for them, and would have found out the facts.'

'And the old man wasn't a Spaniard, but the girl is,' Pirberry observed. 'It was her Bible and her poetry book you found, ma'am, so you said. But it wasn't her Christian name on the fly-leaf.'

'We don't know that. Leda may be David's name for her. Men do give love-names to women, and women to men.'

'Well, I've still to trace the arsenic, ma'am,' said Pirberry, 'before all can turn out for the best. It sounds a long job, after all this time, you know.'

'I can tell you where to find it,' said Mrs Bradley.

'You can.'

'Try the hems of the new silk pennon which Leda put on David's tub, Inspector.'

'But wouldn't that implicate him, ma'am? Or, at any rate, the girl?'

'I don't think so. If you find it, I should say that is proof presumptive that neither of them knows it is there. After all, why should they keep the poison? A pinch or two of arsenic thrown in the river is nobody's business at all. To continue to keep a pennon which is the repository of several lethal doses is to act like a madman, and David and Leda are not mad, whatever else they may be.'

'Then the girl *didn't* write that note?'

'Oh, yes, she did. But the pennon, you remember, was a new one, and I expect, as soon as he got back to the tub he put it straight into the flag locker. I might believe, even then, that David was guilty, but then, if he *had* been guilty, he would not have mentioned so casually that the dead man had been sick before he died.'

'None of it's proof, ma'am. And his finger-prints were certainly on that cistern.'

'But you'd hardly get a summing-up against him, or the girl, on the evidence which you could bring forward at this date.'

Pirberry looked worried and doubtful.

'I'll have to bounce something more out of him,' he said. But before he had the chance to see Harben, there was another extraordinary occurrence, which, in his phrase, "brought the Spaniards right back into the picture". This was nothing less than what seemed to be a wholesale kidnapping of the captain, Estéban, Don Juan and Jorge by the crew of a tug called the *Polly*. El Piojo alone escaped to tell the tale.

The Spaniards, having breakfasted in the Strand, had gone to their Consulate for news of a ship which would repatriate them. Then the captain had been sent for by Pirberry, and after that they had decided to return to the house by the river to see Harben.

He and Leda were preparing to leave, and the first they knew of the developments which followed the return of the Spaniards was supplied by a Quixotic figure, long-limbed, thin and gesticulating, which came running towards them.

It was, as they saw when he approached them, El Piojo.

'Gracias a Dios, señor!' was all that he could find breath to say, as he came up.

'Why, what is the matter, my friend? And where are the others?' asked Harben.

El Piojo put a hand to his heaving chest.

'Taken! Taken!' he cried. 'It is all that villain Don Juan! He has led my noble companions into a trap. Guard yourself, friend. They know you, and are resolved to have your life!'

'Is the captain there?' asked Harben.

'Alas, no! He plunged into the river and is drowned.'

'You saw him jump in?' demanded Leda.

'Yes, certainly, madam. From the bridge of the tug. God's beard! It was terrible! Even Don Juan the traitor has crossed himself when the captain did it.'

'He is safe, then,' said Leda. El Piojo, perceiving, as he thought, a Christian resignation in these words, sympathetically pressed Harben's hand.

Questioned closely, there was little which he could add to what he had said. It appeared that the Spaniards had walked along the riverside path, and, being sailors, had stopped for a bit to watch the tugs and the barges.

A man on a hopper had called out to them, but they could not understand what he said. It appeared, from his gesticulations, that he was inviting them to come on board his craft. They were not so silly, El Piojo reported, as to accept the invitation, for it meant crossing a stretch of thick, black mud. Whilst negotiations were proceeding, another man came up and offered to ferry them across the river to the towing path.

He had a small boat and the captain could understand English sufficiently to make out what he was saying. An agreement was soon arrived at, and the Spaniards embarked all except El Piojo, who decided that there was not room for everyone. He had been upheld in this opinion by the mate, who had given him a shove in the chest and made him cough, and the last El Piojo had seen of his companions was that a large tug, coming up-river towards the old bridge, had slackened, hooted at the ferryboat, and suddenly rammed it. The occupants, including the ferryman, had all been flung into the water. They were picked up, taken on board the tug, and then he saw them being beaten up on her deck by men with clubbed rifles, he thought. The captain, however, had jumped for it from the bridge.

'But it's fantastic!' said Harben. 'You couldn't have seen all that in broad daylight, and on the Thames!'

'We must pick up my brother,' said Leda. She went down the first set of riverside steps she came to, signalled a boatman, and ordered him to row them out to a smart and efficient-looking motor-boat lying at moorings off the eyot.

'That's Mr Welling's cruiser,' said the boatman.

'Yes, yes,' said Harben. '*Cornflower*. I know him. It's quite all right. Get a move on.'

The boatman, feeling himself out-generalled, outnumbered, and not averse to a tip, made no further objections, and rowed them out to the *Cornflower*. Fortunately there was petrol in the tank. Harben, trusting that Mrs Bradley would be able to square matters for him with her friends the police, started up the engine, and almost immediately they had left the island behind them, and were heading for the central span of the bridge.

Past the boatbuilder's yard they went, past the boathouse on the south bank of the river, past the hideous river frontage of the local gasworks, past the willows on the towing-path side, and then El Piojo, crouched on the cabin-top forward, gave a shout and pointed.

'*Es aquí el bote! Veo el remolcador, señor!*'

'I think he can see the tug,' said Leda. The cruiser was coming down opposite the old ferry landing-stage, and a little way past it was a wharf and, beyond this again, a small dock, both of them on the north bank.

The tug had not entered the dock, but was lying hove-to in the entrance. Behind it were three empty barges.

'Doesn't look much wrong,' said Harben, knitting his brows. 'I begin, for the first time, to doubt the good faith of El Piojo.'

Before he could speak to the half-breed, however, a head bobbed up beside the cruiser. The captain's handsome, swarthy face grinned up at them.

'*A perro flaco todo son pulgas!*' he announced, as they dragged him on board.

# CHAPTER TWENTY-THREE

## *Meeting*

Pirberry heard the news of the tug unmoved. He had the name, the *Polly*, and had no doubt that she would soon be traced and apprehended. He was interested, but only mildly so, in the news that Don Juan was on board her.

'The point is, ma'am,' he said to Mrs Bradley, 'fingerprints or no fingerprints, I still see Mr Harben as the murderer of that old man, and the young lady as an accessory either before or after, or before *and* after, the fact. What do you say to that?'

'Nothing,' she replied. 'You may, or may not, be right. Time will show, and, I fancy, it will show very soon.'

'Well, I'd like another word with Mr Harben, ma'am, and I'd like it at once,' said Pirberry.

Mrs Bradley asked permission to be present at the interview.

'You see, sir,' said Pirberry to Harben, 'I can't quite see how I can accept your story.'

'I've told no story,' said Harben, with a reproachful glance at Mrs Bradley.

'Well, sir, suppose you come across with an account of your experiences to the time you first met those Spaniards.'

Harben shrugged.

'You seem to have heard it all,' he said. 'Still, here goes: I took a dislike to an old man in that house in Chiswick you already know about. I broke his neck for him. Then I thought I'd better beat it. That was after I got to know Mrs Bradley, and realized she was wise to what I'd done.

'Meanwhile, the old man's sons were after me. I went to meet his wife, and some chaps went for me – not anyone I knew incidentally. They'd clubbed me, and laid me out before I knew what was what. I remember nothing after that until I came to in an open boat.'

'Nothing? Think, sir. Can't you recollect *anything*?'

He leaned forward, gazing earnestly into the young man's face as though willing him to throw back his mind and find something which would prove to be a clue.

Harben shook his head regretfully.

'I've thought about it until my head swims,' he said. 'There isn't a thing. I can only think that those fellows had some connection with the girl I was visiting, but, beyond that, I can't tell you anything at all.'

'Can you describe the two men?'

'Not very well, I'm afraid. Beyond the fact that they were wearing seamen's caps and that the first one badly needed a shave . . .'

'Could you identify them?'

'I doubt it. I could try. But how are you going to dig them out, when I can't give you anything to go on?'

'We may have dug them out already, sir. That'll be for you to say. They are certainly the fellows that carried you off in the cistern, and it's more than likely they knocked you on the head first.'

'Cistern?' said Harben, startled. 'And what about the Spaniards? You don't connect them with the cistern?'

'We've nothing to go on there, sir.'

Mrs Bradley took up the running.

'Suppose Mr Harben does not identify the two men he's going to be shown? What then, Mr Pirberry?'

'I don't know, ma'am.'

'And suppose he *does* identify them?'

'We pull them in, frighten them, and charge them with attempted murder and abduction.'

'I am most anxious to see how you react to Mr Hankin and Mr Brent,' said Mrs Bradley to Harben.

But Harben did not react at all to Mr Hankin and Mr Brent, although they themselves were ready enough to acknowledge that he was the gentleman they had carried down to the river in the cistern.

'Dumped him on board a little tug that was due to unload by Tower Bridge,' said Hankin, with an appearance of frankness and naïveté which Mrs Bradley appreciated.

'Croak that guy?' said Brent, in righteous indignation, when he had decided that his comrade had made a good impression. 'Sure we never tried to croak him! Me, I don't go croaking anyone, without I am in bad in a saloon. As for this poor guy here, I never seen him except looking good and dead in that square can we toted down to the river. Gosh darn it! What do you cops take us for? We ain't no croakers.'

'Of course not,' said Pirberry. 'All right. Mr Harben says he isn't charging you with anything – this time. But you boys take my tip and get yourselves a nice berth on an oil-tanker. It'll be safer for you, in the end. Gosh darn it!' he added, in peevish involuntary quotation of Mr Brent when the two seamen had gone. 'I suppose you are sure of your facts, sir? You really couldn't recognize these men?'

'I know positively that those are not the men I saw in that house,' said Harben flatly.

'Then I don't know what to do next,' said Pirberry, 'except, of course, we shall want your co-operation over the young lady, sir. Could you tell us her name, by the way?'

'No,' said Harben. 'I'm sorry, but I never heard it – except her Christian name.'

'I see, sir. Well, now, about this young lady, sir, if you don't mind me taking you over your story again. She came to you out of the blue, as it were, one night about twelve months ago. Right?'

'Nearer fifteen months now. It was at the beginning of June. Anyway, Whit Monday night.'

'You admit, of course, sir, that she was by then no stranger to you? In fact, you were in love with her? In fact, she was the wife you mentioned just now? In fact, you *do* know her name?'

'Yes, all right, I admit it.'

'Now, you returned to the lady's house with her in the early morning, to see, as you supposed, the dead body of her husband. Right?' said Pirberry.

'Quite correct.'

'You having already been there once and moved the body. May I ask, sir, what was your feeling when the body proved not to be there on the bed to which you had moved it?'

'Well, I was almost dumbfounded. I mean, I had just concluded it would be exactly as I had left it, and when it wasn't I – well, I couldn't believe the evidence of my eyes.'

'Did you suspect that the lady herself had removed it?'

'No, I didn't. Mrs Bradley asked me something of the sort, but I don't think it had occurred to me for an instant.'

'Can you explain why not, sir?'

'Well, to begin with, you – one doesn't think of young girls removing dead bodies. Secondly, I should say he was much too heavy and awkward for her to lift. Thirdly, I don't honestly see when she could have done it.'

'Yes she was up before you were, sir (if I had the story correctly from Mrs Bradley), on the morning following the death.'

'Yet, that's true. She was. But she only went swimming, you know.'

'We have only your supposition, sir, to go on. Do you know at what time she went swimming?'

'Well, no, I don't. But I think I should have wakened up if she'd come in again before she went swimming, and after she'd moved the body, don't you know.'

'Can you explain that, please?'

'Well, yes. She swam naked. She couldn't have gone naked up to the house. She must have come back to the boat and taken off her clothes if she'd gone up to the house and moved the body first. I know she didn't move it later on. We were in the water together.'

'You can swear to that, sir? She couldn't have gone back to your boat, got dressed, and then slipped up to the house whilst you were still having your swim?'

'Utterly impossible, Inspector. I know she couldn't have gone then. And afterwards, of course, we had breakfast, and went together to the house.'

'Yes sir? And now, sir, another point, please. Did she know any of the neighbours, so far as you could gather?'

'As far as I could gather – but, mind, I'm not committing myself to this! – I should say that she did not – at that time. She uses the next-door air-raid shelter now.'

'Very well, sir. And now, sir, you remember that, while the two of you were in the house that time when you found the body had been moved, the lady made some excuse to get away, and actually stole your motor-boat?'

'Well, not stole it. Borrowed it. One couldn't go further than that, because she returned it, you see.'

'What reason do you suppose she had for wanting to make her escape from the neighbourhood so suddenly?'

'Well, I thought at the time that she was scared, and bunked away from a whole lot of unpleasantness – the inquest and all that – following the old man's death. And I suppose she bunked away from me. She must have guessed that I had killed him.'

'But, at the time, sir, the young lady said *she* had killed him. You remember?'

'Yes, of course I remember. But she explained that. She said the old chap had fallen over a stool left out in the bedroom by her carelessness. I suppose it was later, next morning, she tumbled to the truth.'

'Is that exactly what she said, sir? About his having tumbled over the stool?'

'I don't remember exactly what she said, but that is what I gathered.'

'Very well, sir. But, after she had confessed to you that she'd killed him, and after you'd agreed together not to report the death until the morning, the body is moved from the room and cannot be found. How do you account for it, sir?'

'Damn it, I don't have to account for it! It happened; that's all I know.'

'Very well, sir. We come now to the message left on the pennon of your boat and purporting to come from the lady.'

'Purporting?'

'Well, sir,' said Pirberry with patience, 'I submit that we've no evidence the lady wrote that note. She may have done; most probably she did.'

'She certainly did. Why, the whole of our subsequent conversations . . .'

'Ah, yes, sir. What *were* your subsequent conversations? It might be helpful to know. And another thing, sir. That pennon the lady pinned the note to. Where is it now?'

'Still in my flag-locker, I suppose. You can see it any time if you want to. As for our conversations, well,' Harben looked at him hopelessly, 'you see, that's just the trouble. So far as I remember, Leda was going to tell me about the old man, and explain things a bit, but just then those fellows came in, and that's all I know.'

'You think they'd been listening?' asked Pirberry.

'Dashed if I know. It was certainly rather odd that they should have burst in just then.'

'It has never occurred to you, sir, that you might have been decoyed to the house?'

'No. I think Leda was against them, whoever they were, and, in any case, it was quite my own idea to go to the house.'

'Very good, sir, thank you. Now, sir, if I've got it correctly, your story amounts to this: you hit the old gentleman over the head because you were in love with his wife. Somebody took away his body. Later you were assaulted and kidnapped. Is that correct?'

'Yes. You've left out the previous assault made by two men from a rowing boat.'

'And you don't know who these gentlemen could have been, sir?'

'No – not the faintest idea.'


'Do you think Mr Harben will swear to the dressing-gown, ma'am?' asked Pirberry later.

'If you press him hard enough, yes.'

'You mean, I ought to find the young lady, charge her with using the poison, and then watch how he reacts?'

'That would be one way to do it. Another would be to leave him entirely to me.'

'If you say so, ma'am. I don't want to arrest the young lady without just cause. That sort of thing's unprofessional.'

Mrs Bradley cackled, and promised to do what she could. To this end, she returned to the Rest Centre to interview the Supervising Officer.

'You're an artist,' she said. She produced her notebook. 'I

expect you could reproduce this sketch of mine in paint. Is that asking too much? I know how busy you are.'

'Why, this . . .' said he.

'Yes, it is the pattern on the dressing-gown,' she answered. The Rest Centre officers had seen the exhibit shortly after she herself had been shown it.

'Yes, I could do that very easily. You'd want the colours fresh not faded as they are at present, I suppose?'

'I want it to look new.'

'I'll do it as soon as I've done these food returns,' said he. He was as good as his word. By the time Mrs Bradley had had some tea with the Welfare Officer and had looked at the twin babies who had been born in the Rest Centre hospital during one of the raids, he had sketched in his pattern and painted it.

Mrs Bradley took it gratefully, called at Harben's new lodgings, and learnt that he had returned straightway to *The Island*. She found him with the nuns and the boys, making a model yacht. He seemed glad to see her, and, leaving his companions, went with her to the library.

'So you still think Leda killed that old man,' said Mrs Bradley.

'Yes,' he answered. 'Don't you? But I shouldn't tell Pirberry so, of course, and I wish you hadn't.'

'Allowing that she did, how did the body get to Maidenhead Close?'

She showed him the painting which the Supervising Officer had made. He looked at it intently, with a little worried frown.

'Yes, that's the pattern of the dressing-gown,' he admitted.

'And now, what really happened?' asked Mrs Bradley.

'More or less what I told you.'

'How long had you known her before that night on which he died?'

'Oh, all the previous summer. Why, didn't that part ring true?'

'Which part?'

'You know – her first coming up to the tub and tapping on the port-hole. I meant you to think that I'd never met her before.'

'I did think that at first. But I soon saw that you knew far too much about her for that to have been your first meeting.'

'Tell me,' he said. 'Where did I slip up? It's interesting knowing these things.'

Mrs Bradley checked off the points on her yellow fingers.

'It was before the war. Yet you put the light out before you opened the cabin door of the tub. Why? Obviously because you knew, or, at any rate, guessed who was there, and did not want that person silhouetted against the light.'

'I might have thought it was somebody else – not Leda.'

'In that case you would have mentioned it. Then, your first question: *Not* "Who is it?" But, "Is anything the matter?" Her answer: *Not,* "I've killed my husband" (or father, or anybody else you like), but "I've killed *him*." The inference is that you would understand, without further explanation, whom she meant. It is true that you covered this up with your next question, but I'm afraid the game was already given away.'

'You've a marvellous memory,' he said.

'No. A marvellous notebook,' she replied. 'I've studied this case for months, my dear David. It's been tremendously interesting watching you trying to put a rope round your neck.'

'How did you come to guess that the old man was her husband?' he demanded.

'It was necessary, if the whole thing made sense, that it should be so. I can envisage no other relationship between them which will account for the fact that, although you firmly believe she killed that old man, you are perfectly willing to shield her, and, if necessary, go to the gallows in her place. You feel – for authors are connoisseurs in ethics – that, by being her lover, you are responsible, to some extent, for her crime. But would you call her a poisoner?'

'A poisoner? What has poison to do with the business? The old chap was knocked on the head. That's what she meant when she said he fell over the stool.'

'You don't see her as a kind of Madeleine Smith?' She spoke quizzically, but her black eyes were curiously intent as she asked the question.

'No, I don't! And, in any case, the verdict in Madeleine Smith's case was non-Proven.'

'All the same, you have always thought Leda killed that old man. You've admitted that several times to me, although never in front of witnesses.'

'What else *is* there to think?'

'That she didn't,' said Mrs Bradley mildly. 'And, if she didn't, there is no need for you to feel partly responsible, is there? Plug Williams helped to move the body, of course,' she added, after sufficient pause. 'In fact, Plug suggested the Baptist Chapel roof. He's a Welshman, and that means a pillar of the Baptists, I suppose. When we question the ex-furnaceman who's joined the Navy, we shall find that Plug had a key.'

'How on earth did you know about the body being put on the roof, and how did you tumble to Plug?'

'Bennie Lazarus, one of his boxing pupils, told a garbled sort of story that on the night of the raid after which the body was found, Plug's shop and gymnasium were in ruins. They were not. He was trying to cover Plug's real activities that night. But how did you get Plug to help you?'

'Blackmail. I know a lot about Plug.'

Mrs Bradley grinned, and shook her head.

'Why are you so ashamed of the fact that almost everybody you know will do anything for you?' she said. 'And now what about Hankin and Brent?'

'I don't know them. They are the fellows that Pirberry expected me to swear to.'

'You do know them, David. I happen to know that it was not you, but the dead man who was put into the empty cistern which Hankin and Brent carried down to the river and put on board your boat.'

'I haven't the faintest idea what you're talking about,' he said, 'and as for Plug's activities on that particular night, they had nothing to do with anything criminal.'

'I know that too. I also know that on your boat the old man was brought to Westminster steps. It was among Bartlemas' barrels that the body came into Soho on a brewer's dray. I imagine, to be lodged among the Otamys, old boy, old boy. Who taught the parrot his stuff, if it wasn't you?'

Harben stared at her, fascinated.

'Just exactly what are you getting at?' he asked.

'I suggest that you *wanted* to kill that old man because you were in love with his wife, but I also know you never would have done it. You have admitted that you thought the deed had been done by the wife, Leda, and I suggest that you, with the assistance of Hankin and Brent, took the body down to the river, shipped it on board the tub, brought it to Soho, and then, with Plug's assistance, lodged it on the roof of the Rest Centre (then the roof of the Baptist Church). Later, you thought it ought to be moved, in case it should come down into the Rest Centre during one of the raids. You took a certain amount of risk to get it into the basement and under one of the arches, and there it might have remained, perhaps for years. Plug Williams, knowing the building, and being in possession of keys, assisted you, although *how*, I don't know.'

'Well, it was fairly simple, and, if you asked the right questions at the Rest Centre, no doubt you would find it checked. Plug was helping move their stores from the Section House where they were at first. It was quite simple to bring the old man in his box off the roof at a time when everyone was busy, and to carry it into the basement with a couple of boxes of medical supplies on top. It wasn't so frightfully heavy. We dumped it down in a corner, and watched our chance. Needless to say, Plug had no idea what it was. He thought it the proceeds of a robbery, I think. He used his keys to open the door to the area when nobody else was about, and through we went. And that's about all, I think. It was just a bit of bad luck that blast should have dislodged the beastly thing, and brought it into view.'

'As simple as all that,' said Mrs Bradley. Harben shrugged.

'And if you're wondering why the whole business didn't, and doesn't, make me sick,' he added, 'it's because you don't know what that marriage was like for Leda. And, by the way, what was that you were saying just now about poison?'

'The old man was poisoned, not knocked on the head,' said Mrs Bradley. 'Well, since you are determined to be hanged, go, then, and make your farewells.' She cackled harshly. Harben looked at her in wonder. His colour had gone, and that, with his candid brow, clear eyes and boyishly tousled hair, gave his face an appearance of youthful beauty and heart-rending innocent immaturity.

'Be off with you,' said Mrs Bradley, giving him a push. 'And make up your mind to confess that it was Don Juan who attacked both you and his brother, the Spanish captain.'

His colour began to come back.

'She didn't do it, then,' he said. 'She couldn't have poisoned him. That wouldn't have been her way. She couldn't have done that, could she?'

'You know her better than I do,' said Mrs Bradley. 'You'd better go and see her again.'

He spent the afternoon overhauling the tub, and put off gently in the evening to drop down to the house by the river.

The most curious sense possessed him when darkness fell. It seemed to him that the past was there again, and that, did he but know how to live, the heaven of the future was assured. He thought of Sister Mary Dominic; of his books, and of how much better they might have been. He thought of Leda's fingers gently tap-tapping on the tub; and was startled to hear them, at just after midnight, tap-tapping again against the port-hole.

He went out to the well of his boat. It was moonlight again. Except for the change in the time of year and the snap of autumn coldness in the air, it might have been a repetition of that former night, fifteen months earlier. The ancient river maintained its steady flow; still, on the further bank, on and beyond the island, were the willows, in fuller, darker leaf, but whispering, still with the night wind rustling their leaves. On the near side, still stood the almshouses, sheltering the Six Old men. There were also the steep-hulled hoppers, black and void in the moonlight; the tiny ripple of the river where the tide stirred under the wash of the greenish light; the yachts laid by; the stretches of ooze and slimy stones; the gayer pebbles, the half-buried chains green-weeded and rusted from countless unhurrying tides; and now the fingers, tapping, urgent and quiet; a woman's fingers, saying with gentle pleading:

'Let me in! I am here! Let me in!'

He could fancy his own reply – the reply of his heart – as he went out into the well and leaned over the side. His thoughts, because of his training and natural bent, ran often upon quotation.

> Who knocks? – I who was beautiful
> Beyond all dreams to restore;
> I from the root of the dark thorn am hither,
> And knock on the door.

But, although he climbed over the side and walked half-round the tub, there was nobody there. A chill crept into his bones. He could feel the hair rising on his neck. What if it were true? What if the poem were not of the fabric of moonshine?

The moonlight fell in a shower of greenish-gold like Leda's hair; it washed on the waters like her body; it gleamed in narrow crannies on the green, bright stones like the flecks in her narrow green eyes; it embraced the land in spite of itself, as her arms could embrace a lover; but it was a traitor, as she was; it changed and faded, failed to keep tryst, as she did. Even as he was turning to clamber into the well, a shadow came over the moon and blotted it out.

On an inexplicable impulse, he turned back, and scrambled for the shore. By the time had had reached the house the moon had emerged again. He raced up the nine steps and thundered upon the door. There was a pause. Then a voice from within, which made his heart leap, asked:

'Who comes?'

'David,' he answered. 'Let me in.'

She let him in quickly and shut the door behind him. She took him into a room and thrust him into a chair.

'Has she found out? Are you running away?' she asked.

'Then you knew all the time he was poisoned?'

'Yes, of course I knew. Juan told me almost at once.'

'Told you? Then – '

'Then you didn't do it, David? And you thought all the time – ' She put her long hands on his head. She pushed back his hair with her thumbs, and kissed his eyelids, his throat and his mouth; and, lastly, she pressed her thumbs upon his eyelids as men press coins on the sightless eyes of the dead.

'It was Juan,' she said. 'I should have known.'

'How do you mean – it was Juan?

'He gave me the pennon before he went away. He told me to see that you got it. He always hated you, David, because I loved you. Brothers are like that, sometimes. I had nowhere to put that note, but I had the pennon. I put it on the boat – it was not your boat and it had no flag at the stern – and then I pinned on the note. *Why* did he send you the pennon? When we know that, we know all.'

'We'd better have a look at it,' said Harben. 'It's still in the locker on the tub.'

'It will keep until morning,' she said; and took his hand to lead him up the stairs.

An undercurrent of murder . . .

# THE DARK STREAM

**June Thomson**

The small, peaceful Essex village of Wynford was the sort of place featured on postcards of genteel rural England. So when Stella Reeve was found drowned in the stream which skirted the little community, everyone was sure it was just a tragic accident.

But to Inspector Finch, there was a taint of violence about the scene. He couldn't rationalise it but he could sense it almost as if it were an odour in the air. But even if his intuition was sound he'd need a very clear head to follow the swirling, shifting eddies of motive, intrigue and guile which lay behind this extraordinary case . . .

**'Neatly plotted and trimly told'** *Punch*

Also by June Thomson in Sphere Books:
SHADOW OF A DOUBT
SOUND EVIDENCE
TO MAKE A KILLING
A DYING FALL

0 7221 8441 7    CRIME    £2.75

# THE MAN WHO STOLE THE
# Mona Lisa

## MARTIN PAGE

'I imagine you want me to steal the *Mona Lisa* from the Louvre.'

Morgan felt a pimple above his left nostril about to burst.

'Otherwise, John Pierpont Morgan would hardly go to such inconvenience, and risk such potential embarrassment, to meet the man with the reputation as the world's most skilled thief. Why else would you do that, except to have me steal the world's most valuable object?'

Paris, 1911: somehow, someone achieves the impossible. Only one man could be so audacious, so ingenious, so meticulous a subversive, such a master of disguise and strategy, so silver-tongued to pull off the crime of the century . . .

**'Outrageous . . . *marvellously plotted, line by line it's fascinating*' Los Angeles Times**

0 7474 0031 8    CRIME    £2.75

**A selection of bestsellers from SPHERE**

**FICTION**

| | | |
|---|---|---|
| DAUGHTERS | Suzanne Goodwin | £3.50 ☐ |
| REDCOAT | Bernard Cornwell | £3.50 ☐ |
| WHEN DREAMS COME TRUE | Emma Blair | £3.50 ☐ |
| THE LEGACY OF HEOROT | Niven/Pournelle/Barnes | £3.50 ☐ |
| THE PHYSICIAN | Noah Gordon | £3.99 ☐ |

**FILM AND TV TIE-IN**

| | | |
|---|---|---|
| COMING TOGETHER | Alexandra Hine | £2.99 ☐ |
| RUN FOR YOUR LIFE | Stuart Collins | £2.99 ☐ |
| BLACK FOREST CLINIC | Peter Heim | £2.99 ☐ |
| INTIMATE CONTACT | Jacqueline Osborne | £2.50 ☐ |
| BEST OF BRITISH | Maurice Sellar | £8.95 ☐ |

**NON-FICTION**

| | | |
|---|---|---|
| THE COCHIN CONNECTION | Alison and Brian Milgate | £3.50 ☐ |
| HOWARD & MASCHLER ON FOOD | Elizabeth Jane Howard and Fay Maschler | £3.99 ☐ |
| FISH | Robyn Wilson | £2.50 ☐ |
| THE SACRED VIRGIN AND THE HOLY WHORE | Anthony Harris | £3.50 ☐ |
| THE DARKNESS IS LIGHT ENOUGH | Chris Ferris | £4.50 ☐ |

*All Sphere books are available at your local bookshop or newsagent, or can be ordered direct from the publisher. Just tick the titles you want and fill in the form below.*

Name_____

Address_____

_____

Write to Sphere Books, Cash Sales Department, P.O. Box 11, Falmouth, Cornwall TR10 9EN

Please enclose a cheque or postal order to the value of the cover price plus:

UK: 60p for the first book, 25p for the second book and 15p for each additional book ordered to a maximum charge of £1.90.

OVERSEAS & EIRE: £1.25 for the first book, 75p for the second book and 28p for each subsequent title ordered.

BFPO: 60p for the first book, 25p for the second book plus 15p per copy for the next 7 books, thereafter 9p per book.

*Sphere Books reserve the right to show new retail prices on covers which may differ from those previously advertised in the text elsewhere, and to increase postal rates in accordance with the P.O.*